A Lady's Laughter

Miss Barlow laughed then, and Rivendale found himself catching his breath. When was the last time he had heard a lady laugh? Particularly at something he said? When had he even looked to see if he could make a lady laugh? In the months since his wife's death, he had taken on a grim and sober mien that was, in its own way, perhaps as daunting as Anna's withdrawal from the world.

So now he found himself smiling, and experienced no little surprise at how good it felt. He was even more surprised to find himself wondering if he could make Miss Barlow laugh again.

The Widower's Folly

❧

April Kihlstrom

A SIGNET BOOK

SIGNET
Published by New American Library, a division of
Penguin Putnam Inc., 375 Hudson Street,
New York, New York 10014, U.S.A.
Penguin Books Ltd, 27 Wrights Lane,
London W8 5TZ, England
Penguin Books Australia Ltd, Ringwood,
Victoria, Australia
Penguin Books Canada Ltd, 10 Alcorn Avenue,
Toronto, Ontario, Canada M4V 3B2
Penguin Books (N.Z.) Ltd, 182–190 Wairau Road,
Auckland 10, New Zealand

Penguin Books Ltd, Registered Offices:
Harmondsworth, Middlesex, England

First published by Signet, an imprint of New American Library,
a division of Penguin Putnam Inc.

First Printing, July 2001
10   9   8   7   6   5   4   3   2   1

Copyright © April Kihlstrom, 2001

All rights reserved

Ⓢ REGISTERED TRADEMARK—MARCA REGISTRADA

Printed in the United States of America

PUBLISHER'S NOTE
This is a work of fiction. Names, characters, places, and incidents either are the product of the author's imagination or are used fictitiously, and any resemblance to actual persons, living or dead, business establishments, events, or locales is entirely coincidental.

BOOKS ARE AVAILABLE AT QUANTITY DISCOUNTS WHEN USED TO PROMOTE PRODUCTS OR SERVICES. FOR INFORMATION PLEASE WRITE TO PREMIUM MARKETING DIVISION, PENGUIN PUTNAM INC., 375 HUDSON STREET, NEW YORK, NEW YORK 10014.

*This book is dedicated
to the memory of Melinda Helfer.
She loved Regencies, and she believed
in my books when I needed that
belief most. I will miss her.*

Chapter 1

Miss Theresa Barlow drew in her breath and stared at the neatly tied-up manuscript in her hand. Surely Mr. Plimpton would like her latest effort. He had raved about the first one and that printing had sold well, and she knew this one was just as good.

Still, Tessa could not help but worry. She loved the stories she wrote. She thought sometimes that she loved the worlds she created more than the one in which she lived. She didn't think she could bear it if Mr. Plimpton didn't like this latest story. Well, she told herself, there was only one way to find out.

Perhaps if Aunt Margaret, Miss Winsham, had not stopped Tessa as she was about to go out the door, matters would have gone differently. Perhaps if Tessa had chosen a different day to call upon her publisher, matters would have gone differently. But the manuscript was done, and Tessa was eager to hear what Mr. Plimpton would say about it. And Margaret did stop her at the door.

"My dear, I have something for you," she said.

Tessa suppressed her exasperation with difficulty. "Can it not wait?" she asked.

"I can't explain why, but I think perhaps you need this now," Miss Winsham persisted.

Tessa sighed and set down the manuscript, then turned to her aunt. "What is it?" she asked, as much affection as irritation in her voice.

"This locket."

"Alex's locket? But I thought she lost it," Tessa said, bewildered.

"It is your mother's locket, to be precise," Miss Winsham replied. "And yes, Alexandra had it, then lost it. I found it, and now it is time for you to have it," she said, handing it to her niece.

"But Alex—" Tessa began.

"Alexandra has no further need of the locket. It is your turn." Miss Winsham paused, then relented. "In our family, this locket is passed to each sister in turn," she explained. "And then, after they have no more need of it, it goes to the daughters in the family. First it was your sister's turn, and now it is yours. For your mother's sake, take it and wear it, as Alexandra did before you."

And what was there to say to that? So, just as her older sister had once done, Tessa took the locket and turned it over and read the inscription: "Wish Always With Love."

And just as Alexandra had once asked, Tessa said, "What does this mean?"

Miss Winsham hesitated. "I suppose it is all foolishness," she said reluctantly, "but you are supposed to wish for what you want most in your life and then open the locket."

Tessa looked at her aunt oddly, but then she dutifully stared at the closed locket. What did she most want in her life? For everyone to read her stories to their children, of course, or for the children to read the stories themselves.

But she wanted much more than that. Tessa wanted someone to hold her as she read her stories aloud to her own children. And despite Alexandra's success in finding Sir Robert Stamford, marriage did not seem a likely possibility. After all, what man would want a woman without a dowry? A woman, moreover, who spent her days hunched over paper with quill in hand because she found the worlds she created safer and more appealing than the world around her?

Still, with a wistful feeling in her heart, Tessa opened the locket. For a brief moment a man's face appeared. It was a very handsome face, and that made it all the more absurd, for what would such a man ever want with her? She felt odd, almost a little dizzy.

And then the image abruptly disappeared. Tessa blinked. She looked again. Nothing. The locket was empty. She closed the locket and opened it again. Still nothing.

"What was that?" she murmured and looked to Miss Winsham for the answer.

The older woman sighed. "Once I would have said it was all nonsense," she said slowly. "A trick of the imagination, nothing more. But your sister saw Stamford's face in the locket. And that came true. So perhaps there is something to the legend. Though I still have my doubts. I suppose you saw a face as well?"

Tessa nodded slowly. "Yes, I saw a man's face—the face of a very handsome man. Tell me what it means."

With what sounded like both exasperation and longing in her voice, Miss Winsham answered, "The legend says that when the locket is yours and you hold it, as yours, for the first time and wish, when you open it you will see the face of the man you are to marry. I thought it nonsense. I saw a face once and he never appeared, so the legend does not always come true. Perhaps it never comes true and those who think it does are only fooling themselves."

Tessa was silent for several moments, her imagination racing with ideas. Finally, she asked another question that Alex had asked, with the same wariness in her voice, "Did my mother see my father's face?"

Miss Winsham hesitated again. "No," she said reluctantly. "She told me she saw another. A man our parents refused to let her marry."

"Good!" Tessa's voice was brisk. "I was very little when Mama died, but I remember how unhappy she always was. I should hate to think that Papa was *her* destiny."

Resolutely, Tessa fastened the locket around her neck. In the same brisk voice, she said to her aunt, "I must go. Mr. Plimpton is waiting for this manuscript and I must deliver it to him today."

"You ought to take a footman," Miss Winsham told her niece bluntly.

Tessa laughed. "To be sure, if I were a young girl I would. But I am four and twenty, Aunt Margaret. Surely old enough to go out and about on my own!"

And then, before her aunt could raise any further objections, Tessa sailed out the front door and down the steps to where Sir Robert's coachman was waiting. Her sister's husband was most generous, allowing Tessa, Lisbeth, and Aunt Margaret to stay in his town house, providing a carriage for their use, and showing them all sorts of other kindnesses. Though she and her sisters had once sworn never to marry, a man like Sir Robert could almost cause one to regret such a vow, Tessa thought wistfully.

And as she rode to the publisher, she clutched the locket in her hand and felt it grow warm under her touch. She missed Mama. She supposed she always would. Where Papa had been an angry, and even at times, frightening parent, Mama had been all warmth and love and the scent of rose water.

William, Lord Rivendale stared at his daughter, who, in turn, stared wordlessly out at the street below. The latest expert had just left, and his words had not been encouraging.

"You must come to terms with the fact that the child may never speak," the man had said. "Take her home and simply accept that this is the way she is."

For a moment, just a moment, Rivendale was tempted to do as the expert said, and go home. He missed the people he knew there, he missed the things he had done when he was home. He had come to London to consult the best possible men, and he had done just that, but it hadn't done any good. Anna still did not speak. So perhaps it was time to go home.

But that sentiment only lasted a moment before Rivendale shook himself impatiently. He could not take Anna home—not when he was unable to face the place himself. Not when the memories there still haunted him and must, therefore, haunt his daughter as well. No, he could not do that to either of them. They would stay in London. There must be someone else he could consult, something else he could try!

Because he was angry with himself for contemplating for even a moment, returning to his home estate, Rivendale looked about him for distraction. His gaze settled on his daughter's nurse. The woman shrugged helplessly. He wanted to shake her, but he didn't. He knew it was not her fault. She had tried to reach Anna, just as he had. It was not her fault that both of them had failed.

Beside him, William's oldest friend, Lord Thomas Kepley, cleared his throat. "Deuced shame," he said.

Rivendale nodded, not trusting himself to speak. He had asked Kepley to be here so that he would not have to face the news alone—whatever it might be. But he found his friend's company small comfort right now.

"You mustn't give up," Kepley went on, his voice low but strong. "She is a beautiful child and one day, when she has reason enough, she will speak again."

Rivendale looked at his daughter. She was beautiful. But she would not speak. What on earth would give her reason enough to do so if she had not found one in the whole past year? William asked himself. It was hopeless! Then his eyes fell on the book beside his daughter.

Anna was too young to read, but she loved this new book Rivendale had bought her, loved to have it read to her. It was a fanciful tale, written by a lady of quality, or so the publisher claimed. No doubt the author was a grandmoth-

erly creature, whose own children were grown and out of
the house and who now had the leisure, and the desire, to
write down the stories she had once told her own children.

A notion occurred to William. He went very still as he
considered his idea. He' was not the sort of man to stand
around and wait for things to happen. He did not intend to
do so now, either. He had exhausted every other possibility,
so why not explore this one?

"I am going out," he told Anna's nurse brusquely.

"Want company?" Kepley asked.

Rivendale hesitated, then shook his head. "No, I think it
best that I do this alone."

Good friend that he was, Kepley did not argue but
merely clapped Rivendale on the shoulder and took his
leave. Twenty minutes later, William stood in the office of
the man who had published the book his daughter loved.
Mr. Plimpton was being decidedly difficult.

"I am very sorry, Lord Rivendale, but I cannot tell you
the name of the author, nor give you her direction."

"You do not understand," William persisted, his voice
quiet but firm. "My daughter does not speak, but perhaps if
the author would come and talk to her it would make a difference. That is all I ask, that she come and speak to my
daughter. I simply wish you to ask her if she would be willing to do so."

Mr. Plimpton hesitated, and it was as though Rivendale
could read his mind. His lordship was precisely the sort of
well-breeched customer who could send a great deal of
business his way, or withhold it if he chose, Mr. Plimpton
would be thinking. The sort of customer one ought to
oblige. But someone had no doubt made it clear that he, or
she, would not be pleased if Mr. Plimpton passed on the author's name and direction to anyone. Patently he, or she,
was also the sort of person one did not offend.

With very carefully chosen words, Mr. Plimpton said to
the gentleman before him, "I can give you neither her name

nor her direction. Nor will I risk distressing her by passing on your request. You must understand, you are not the only one who wishes to place a claim on her time, her attention, and her good nature."

Lord Rivendale leaned forward. He resisted the temptation to slam his fist upon the desk. Instead he said in a voice of command that had drawn him respect even when he was still a young boy, "I need to speak with her."

"Sir, I cannot help you. I believe, however, that she is to deliver a manuscript today. I cannot point her out to you or introduce you but . . ."

Mr. Plimpton left the rest of the suggestion unspoken, but Lord Rivendale caught the meaning at once. He drew in a deep breath and nodded. "Thank you," he said. "I promise I shall not distress the woman."

"You will please wait outside," Mr. Plimpton said briskly. "I shall not, at any rate, have her disturbed in here."

And so, a few minutes later, William found himself leaning against the building, watching and waiting. It reminded him of all the times he and his cohorts had done just that. But they had been watching for their enemies. This time, he hoped, he was waiting for a friend.

In spite of himself, Rivendale smiled at the foolish analogy. No, this was nothing like then. Now he was waiting for some unknown elderly lady to emerge from a carriage and enter the publisher's offices. When she came out, he would try to speak to her.

So intent was he on the image he had created in his mind that when William thought he saw such a woman coming toward him, he stepped forward. Straight into the path of a young woman with light brown hair, green eyes, and a very pretty smile.

"I am terribly sorry," Rivendale said, reaching out to steady her.

His fingers brushed a sheaf of papers that the lady clutched in her hands, and his eyes focused on a locket at her throat. When he looked at the papers, he saw that they were tied up so that he could glimpse only one word, but it looked to be part of the title of a story. And the word was "dragon." As in: *The Reluctant Dragon*, perhaps? That was, the publisher had announced, to be the title of the next book by the author whose stories Rivendale's daughter adored. The book that Mr. Plimpton promised to everyone who subscribed to the next volumes in advance.

William was so startled that he could only stare, unseeing, at the woman before him. He was so stunned, in fact, that he did not notice she was staring equally intently at him! Finally she shook herself free, and in a voice that did not seem altogether steady she said, "If you will please step aside, sir, I need to go through this doorway."

"I—, yes, of course."

With a very strange look she brushed past him and disappeared into Mr. Plimpton's office. William could not blame the woman for staring at him as if he were some sort of madman. He must have seemed like one, staring at her as he had. But it came as such a shock to see such a young woman, rather than the elderly one he had imagined. Didn't her husband mind that she spent her time writing stories? Didn't he worry what the *ton* would say if she were found out? And, perhaps most important, what would the husband think of what Lord Rivendale wished to ask the lady to do?

So jumbled were his thoughts that William was still blocking the entryway when the young woman emerged from Mr. Plimpton's offices and wished to leave the building. Once again she had to ask him to step aside.

This time he was determined not to lose his chance. As the young woman headed for a nearby carriage, he followed her. In a brisk voice he asked, "Are you the author of *The Shy Unicorn*, ma'am?"

She froze for an instant, and then she began to walk even faster.

"Please, ma'am! If you are I must talk to you! It is about my daughter!"

Perhaps it was the desperation in his voice. Perhaps it was the mention of his daughter. In any event, she paused again, and this time turned to face him. Her clear green eyes seemed to search his face, looking for something to reassure her. In the end she must have found it, for she took a deep breath and nodded. In an unexpectedly brisk voice she answered him.

"Very well. What is it, sir?"

William tried to take her elbow. She stepped away. He stood very still, trying to choose the words that would move her, would stir her compassion. In the end he simply said, "I am Lord Rivendale and I have a daughter who will not speak. The doctors say they can do nothing to help her. She has been this way since my wife, her mother, died, a year ago. The only thing in this past year that has ever captured her attention is your story *The Shy Unicorn*. I thought, I hope, that perhaps if you came to see her, it would make her speak. To ask you about your book, if for no other reason."

She wanted to refuse, he thought. Her upbringing and her common sense must clearly have told her to have nothing to do with this madman who had accosted her on the street. But perhaps her heart was a different matter?

William could see the softening in her eyes, her reluctant, and wistful smile as she listened to his story about his daughter Anna.

"Very well," she said at last. "When would you like me to come and see her?"

"Now!"

The young woman blinked, clearly taken aback. Lord Rivendale almost regretted the impulse that had caused him to say she must talk to his daughter now. But it was too late to take back those words.

Instead of offering another time, he said, his voice low

and urgent, "You must understand! It has been a year since I last heard my daughter speak! I feel as if I have no time to waste. The doctors tell me that the longer she goes without speaking, the less likely she is ever to speak again. My carriage is right over there. I can take you and have you back home in less than an hour."

She heard him out. She took another deep breath. Then, just as he expected her to refuse, she said, "Very well, sir. I shall come and meet your daughter. But I shall go in my own carriage. Please give my coachman the direction of your house and we shall meet you there."

Lord Rivendale gave silent thanks to heaven and hurried to do as she had bidden him.

Chapter 2

Tessa clutched the locket at her throat. She knew it was foolishly improper to do this. Perhaps even a bit mad. Neither her sisters nor Aunt Margaret would have approved. And yet, could any of them have resisted going to the aid of a child in need?

No, any of them would have gone, just as she was going, Tessa thought. Still, she shivered, even though the day was very warm. It wasn't entirely the thought of defying convention, either. Rather it was the odd coincidence that Lord Rivendale resembled so closely the face she thought she had seen in the locket. It was nonsense, of course—wasn't it? Such a thing couldn't be more than foolish coincidence and a lively imagination, could it?

Tessa hoped there would not be a great many people at Lord Rivendale's home. She was not comfortable in such situations, although she thought she hid it well—so well, in fact, that her sisters had no notion what agonies she felt whenever she accompanied them to balls or on social calls. She couldn't let them know, or they would have curtailed their activities for her sake, and she could not let that happen. Not when it brought them such pleasure.

Besides, Tessa was not the sort of woman to give in to her fears. The last thing she would allow was for them to rule her. Still, as her hand clutched the locket at her throat, she could not help hoping there would be almost no one at Lord Rivendale's house.

*　　*　　*

William arrived at his house first. He ran upstairs to find Anna sitting just where he had left her. Her hair was half tangled because she had refused, as usual, to let Nanny finish brushing it out.

"Anna," Rivendale said softly, "someone is coming to see you."

No response. He hadn't really expected one. A little louder he said, "It is the lady who wrote the book. The book you love so much. *The Shy Unicorn.*"

At that his daughter turned. And there was such a bright look in her eyes that it tore at Rivendale's heart. When was the last time he had seen a look of hope, of happiness, in her eyes? Had he ever seen such a look, even before her mother died? If so, he couldn't remember it.

He reached out a hand to her and held his breath as she slipped off her window seat, careful to scoop up the beloved book and bring it with her. She took his hand and meekly let him lead her downstairs.

The footman opened the door just as William and his daughter reached the bottom of the stairs. Both of them stared at their visitor as she stood in the doorway, a halo of bright sunlight around her.

"Lord Rivendale?" the lady asked almost shyly. "Is this your daughter, Anna?"

He nodded, unable to speak, his emotions too full of hope and fear. He watched as the lady knelt down, careless of whether her skirts might gather dust or not. She smiled at Anna and said in a gentle voice, "Hello. I am told you like my story. Would you like me to read it to you?"

For a moment William thought Anna would answer. But in the end she only nodded and held out a hand to the lady. Well, he told himself, trying not to feel disappointed, it was a start. Even with the author of *The Shy Unicorn*, it might take time for Anna to feel safe enough to try to talk.

Rivendale followed as Anna led the lady into the parlor.

It was strange, he thought, but he still did not know her name. He had been so intent on persuading her to come and see Anna that he had not thought to ask. He would rectify that mistake before she left.

He was careful to sit in the corner of the parlor as the lady read to Anna. He did not wish to distract either one of them, not while there was a chance for a miracle. He leaned back in his chair, closed his eyes, and listened to the lilting voice that was almost musical as it read the tale of the unicorn who was even more shy than the rest of its kind. Just like Anna, he thought. Perhaps that was why she loved the story. Because she felt so much like that very special unicorn. If so, he could only hope that just as the shy unicorn found, in the end, someone to trust, Anna would as well.

Certainly she curled up, trustingly enough, next to the lady on the couch. And she reached out, more than once to touch the curls that escaped from beneath the bonnet the lady wore. But was it enough to let her break the self-imposed silence within which she had lived for the past year? Rivendale didn't know, and he was afraid to guess.

He was also afraid of what the lady must be thinking of them. The questions she must have. Questions he wasn't at all sure he wished to try to answer.

But she seemed at ease with Anna. She seemed happy to read to her, and tolerant of the incursions on her person. And that was a blessing for which William found himself profoundly grateful.

Word must have spread throughout the house about the lady, for just as she finished reading the story to Anna, Lord Rivendale's housekeeper appeared. She carried a tray laden with teapot, cups, and a plate of pastries, none of which he had requested. The lady, the authoress, seemed taken aback at the sight of it.

"Oh, but I must be going," she said, hastily rising to her feet.

"Oh, ma'am, I'm sorry," Lord Rivendale's housekeeper

said, the dismay evident in her expression and in her voice.
"I were only thinking that reading might have made you
thirsty, and the wee one never eats enough. I thought she
might try a cake or two if you was to eat one with her."

Anna was thin, William thought, but he had not, heretofore, thought her appetite to be particularly impaired. Still,
the corners of his mouth tugged upward in a smile as his
daughter pulled at the lady's hand and pointed to the tray,
silently pleading.

He could see the reluctance in the lady's eyes, the wariness, and he tried to reassure her. He thought perhaps she
was a bit afraid of being there, and he found himself wanting to take away that fear.

"You must not do anything you do not wish to do,"
Rivendale said, coming to stand near her. "But perhaps another ten minutes would not make you so very late for
whatever appointment you must reach?"

"N-no appointment," she said, blushing charmingly, in
his opinion. "I simply do not wish to impose."

"It is no imposition, but, as my housekeeper has said, a
favor you would be doing us," William assured her.
"Please—you are the first new person Anna has shown any
fondness for, any comfort with, in more than a year."

She looked from him to the housekeeper to Anna, and it
was the child, he knew, who persuaded her. No more than
anyone else in this household could she resist Anna's
haunted brown eyes.

The lady sat back down, and Lord Rivendale's housekeeper set the tray on a table beside her. Then she quickly
vanished, no doubt to regale the other servants belowstairs
about the lady his lordship had brought home—the first
lady, other than his mother, who had set foot in this house
in months.

After she had poured out tea for them, William said to
the author, "You will forgive me, ma'am, but I never

thought to ask your name. And all I know from your book is that you are a lady of quality."

She smiled at that, as he had hoped she would. "I am Miss Barlow," she said.

"Miss?"

She hesitated. "I am staying with my sister and her husband, Sir Robert Stamford. My aunt would say I should not have gone out alone, but I am persuaded I am past the age of needing a chaperone everywhere I go."

Rivendale would have disagreed. He could have told Miss Barlow that she seemed not to be of such an advanced age to him. But if she had not gone out without a chaperone, perhaps he would not have succeeded in persuading her to come home with him, for surely her chaperone would have objected to such an unconventional request, to such unconventional behavior. No, he was not about to argue with her over the matter.

Miss Barlow looked at Anna. "Do they say why your daughter does not speak? Is it perhaps her hearing that has been impaired?"

William shook his head. "We think she hears well enough. After all, she is enthralled when anyone reads your book to her. They say, the experts I have consulted, that perhaps it was the trauma of seeing her mother die. They were out driving, at my country estate, you see. It was an open carriage and we think something must have startled the horses. At any rate, the carriage overturned and my wife was killed. Anna was thrown free, and while she was bruised, no permanent damage occurred—except that she does not speak."

"So Anna saw her mother killed?" Miss Barlow asked. "Poor child! It is no wonder she should have withdrawn into herself. How old is she?"

"Six—old enough for a governess, if she would speak to one. I still have her with Nanny because she has known

Nanny all her life. I did not wish to force one more change on Anna until she has recovered from the last."

Miss Barlow nodded. She looked at Anna, and when she noticed the child staring at her, she reached out and gently stroked her hair.

"I am sorry you have lost your mama," she said in a serious but gentle voice. "I lost my mama when I was not so very much older than you. And I know how dearly that hurt. But I am glad you have a papa who loves and cares for you. That is a very wonderful thing."

Something in her expression, something in the words she chose, made Lord Rivendale want to ask her if her father had loved and cared for her after her mother died. But he did not dare. They did not stand upon such terms that he felt such familiarity would be permissible. So, instead, William spoke of her writing.

"We, like so many others I know, are already subscribed and eagerly await the tale of the reluctant dragon. Is that the manuscript you were delivering to Mr. Plimpton today?"

Miss Barlow smiled. "Yes, it was. It took me a little longer than expected to complete, and he was perhaps a trifle premature in promising the publication date he did. But I am glad your daughter likes my work."

"Not only my daughter," Rivendale protested. "I, too, found myself enthralled by the tale of that poor unicorn. And I expect to be just as enthralled with the next."

She colored up then, and looked away from him. There was some constraint in her voice as she said, "You are very kind, perhaps too kind, to say so."

"And you dislike the attention?" William hazarded shrewdly.

Now she looked at him again. In a manner calculated to depress pretensions she said firmly, "I dislike effusive compliments. I prefer honesty in all things."

"I spoke the truth," Rivendale answered austerely. "But since it distresses you, Miss Barlow, I shall speak of it no more. Just know that in this house your work is very much appreciated. And I promise," he added, unbending a little so there was a hint of mischief in his voice, "that the moment I cease to think so, I shall be sure to tell you."

She laughed then, and Rivendale found himself catching his breath. When was the last time he had heard a lady laugh? Particularly at something he said? When had he even looked to see if he could make a lady laugh? In the months since his wife's death, he had taken on a grim and sober mien that was, in its own way, perhaps as daunting as Anna's withdrawal from the world.

So now he found himself smiling, and experienced no little surprise at how good it felt. He was even more surprised to find himself wondering if perhaps he could cause Miss Barlow to laugh again.

But she did not give him the chance. She rose to her feet and held out her hand to him. "Thank you, Lord Rivendale," she said, "for inviting me to your home. And for letting me meet your daughter, Anna. I wish her the best, and hope that she may soon find her tongue. And I wish you the best as well. I hope you may find answers, both for her and for yourself, for your own grief."

And then Miss Barlow turned to leave. Lord Rivendale wanted to hold on to her hand, but instead he let it go, knowing he would only frighten her if he did not. Somehow he knew she was more easily frightened than she liked anyone to know. But by the time she reached the foyer, he found his tongue.

"Will you come again?" he asked.

She looked past him at Anna, who had followed them. "I don't know," she said. "You can see that it made no difference, my coming here. She still did not speak."

"Yes, but she is happier than I have seen her since before her mother's death," William said, with more than a hint of desperation in his voice. "Please come again? For both our sakes."

Miss Barlow was weakening, Rivendale thought. He could feel it. Just as he could feel the moment she steeled herself to refuse. And how could he blame her? He was a stranger—someone who had forced himself to her attention and dragged her to his home on a fool's errand. Except that he hoped it was not a fool's errand. But how was either of them to know, if she did not come again?

In the end, it was Anna who resolved the matter. As Miss Barlow and Lord Rivendale stood staring at one another uncertainly. Anna went up to Miss Barlow and tugged on her hand. Miss Barlow knelt down to look the child in the eye.

"What is it, Anna?" she asked.

As William watched, a lump in his throat, Anna pleaded silently with her eyes.

"Do you want me to come again?" Miss Barlow asked, sounding as if she spoke the words against her will.

Anna's face lit up in a bright smile, and she nodded her head so vigorously that there could be no doubt about what she wished she could say.

Miss Barlow looked up at Lord Rivendale, and both amusement and dismay showed in her fine green eyes. She looked back at Anna, and after what seemed an interminable wait, smiled and said, "Very well, I shall come again. But you must do what your papa tells you, all right?"

Again Anna nodded vigorously. William reached out a hand to help Miss Barlow to her feet. She took it, and this time did not object when he did not instantly let go.

"I am grateful," he said.

"And I am clearly fallen prey to your daughter's large brown eyes," Miss Barlow retorted, her smile belying the sharpness of her words.

"As are we all, in this house."

She nodded. "Yes, of course you would be," she said, sympathy evident in both her voice and her face. "Shall we say one week from today? Is this a good time of day for Anna?"

"One week from today, this time, would be fine," Rivendale answered.

He resisted the urge to beg her to return on the morrow. Nor did he, despite an absurd impulse not to let Miss Barlow leave, interfere as she went out the front door to her waiting carriage.

Lady Stamford's sister, eh? Lord Rivendale considered what he knew of Sir Robert Stamford and decided that he would need to be careful where Miss Barlow was concerned.

Chapter 3

"Lord Rivendale, eh?" Sir Robert Stamford said to his wife's sister. "I have heard of the man. They say he has been something of a recluse since his wife died. But he is, by all accounts, an honorable fellow."

"Yes, but do you think it wise for my sister to visit there? At his house?" Alexandra, Lady Stamford asked with some anxiety. "You know how it will look, what people will say, if they discover she is going there."

"I cannot very well demand that Lord Rivendale bring his daughter here—it would be most improper of me to be so forward!" Tessa protested. "And if you had seen the poor child, Alex, with her haunted eyes, you would understand why I cannot refuse the man such a simple favor."

"Well, I should like it if he did come here," Lisbeth, her younger sister, pronounced. "Then we could decide what we think of the fellow."

"It doesn't matter what we think of Lord Rivendale, or what Tessa thinks of the man. Does it?" Miss Winsham asked, looking sharply at her niece. "You are simply trying to help his daughter, correct?"

Tessa hesitated. How could she tell her sisters, or her aunt, that she thought she had seen Lord Rivendale's face in the locket? How could she tell them that that occurrence, that coincidence, more than anything else, was the reason she had agreed to go to his house to meet his daughter. It was all nonsense, wasn't it? She couldn't have really seen a face, could she? Surely it was just her fevered imagination.

Aloud, however, all she said was, "You are all of you being very foolish. No one knows I go to Lord Rivendale's house, so it cannot harm my reputation."

"What if someone sees you?" Alexandra demanded.

Tessa took a deep breath. "Very well, Alex, if it will set your mind at ease, I shall suggest that Lord Rivendale bring his daughter here. If, that is, he even presumes to ask me to read to her again."

"He will," Lisbeth predicted. "If he is so concerned about his daughter's welfare, he will no doubt ask you to see her every week. And if you don't want to go help her, I should be happy to try!"

"It is not your stories the child wishes to hear," Miss Winsham said sharply. "It is Theresa's."

Lisbeth shot her aunt a rebellious glare, but she did not protest any further. Tessa inwardly sighed. Her younger sister was bored, and it was scarcely surprising. There was very little for her to do, especially now that the Season was over.

To be sure, London was not entirely devoid of ladies and gentlemen. Certainly her sister Alex and Sir Robert still received invitations. They took Tessa and Lisbeth with them whenever they could. But neither Tessa nor her sister had any great fondness for social engagements with people they did not know.

In any event, Tessa thought, simply being in London must remind Lisbeth of her one Season—just at it reminded Tessa of hers. And she could not think that Lisbeth would want to remember that time any more than she did. To have had a father determined to sell his daughters to the highest bidder—for that had been the honest truth—could not imbue such memories with anything other than disfavor.

What Lisbeth needed, Tessa thought, was a focus for her energies, just as she had her writing and Alex had her mar-

riage. But other than caring for children, there was very little Lisbeth liked to do.

Well, perhaps tonight would be entertaining. They were
supposed to go to a musical evening at some lady or other's
house. Perhaps in listening to the music both Tessa and her
sister Lisbeth could forget their boredom.

Lord Rivendale cursed himself for a fool, and he cursed
his friend Kepley even stronger, as he tried yet again to tie
his cravat properly. How long had it been since he had worried this way about such matters? How long since anyone
had expected him to do so? How long since he had accepted invitations from anyone other than Kepley?

No doubt the sight of him at tonight's musical event
would cause a stir. And for at least the hundredth time he
wondered if he was foolish to go. Just because he had overheard someone say that Sir Robert Stamford and his bride
and her sisters would be there—just because Miss Barlow
would be there.

He could not have explained, even to himself, why he
wished to see her tonight. He knew she would be coming to
visit Anna again and he would see her then. Why, therefore,
was he so impatient that he must subject himself to the gossip his appearance would be certain to cause, and to the bad
music his hostess was notorious for arranging?

He said as much aloud when Kepley arrived to accompany him to the party. Kepley leaned on his cane and
laughed. "They will say it is time and past that you came
out of hiding," he countered bluntly. "And they will wonder
why you did not do so before. Besides, you are there to act
as my shield. Damned if I know why a battlefield injury
should seem romantic to the ladies, but it does. Either that
or repulses 'em badly. Either way, you are going to protect
me from the ones who want to coo over me and the ones
who think I shouldn't show myself in polite company."

"Oh, to be sure, as if you have ever needed a protector!" Rivendale joked.

Kepley didn't answer him, but merely met William's eyes in a steady gaze, reminding both of them of the times they had each come to the other's rescue over the years, starting when they were little boys.

Rivendale grumbled, but despite all his doubts, he and Kepley presented themselves to their hostess at the appointed time. And if Rivendale's eyes darted about looking for a certain young lady, still he managed to answer his hostess's questions properly and charm her into a smile as he complimented both her appearance and that of the daughter she was trying so desperately to launch.

Some whispered behind their fans as he passed, but others greeted Rivendale as if he had never been absent from society. They spoke as naturally as if they saw him at such events every night. Soon he began to regret the grief that had caused him to isolate himself from his friends for such a long time.

Indeed, so caught up was William in renewing old friendships that he would not have noticed the entrance of Miss Barlow and her party if one of the men he was speaking with had not pointed them out.

"There's Stamford. And his bride. Salvaged his position with Prinny, you know."

"Who are the young ladies with them?" another gentleman asked.

"Haven't you heard? Lady Stamford has two sisters. Quite lovely, if a bit older than one would expect. Gather their father tried unsuccessfully to fire them off a few years ago and then washed his hands of the attempt. Been buried in the country ever since."

Rivendale turned, careful not to appear more interested than any of the other men about him. If Miss Barlow had looked attractive dressed in a deep blue walking dress the other morning, she looked even more appealing in tonight's swirling confection of soft green silk.

Behind him, the others were still talking.

"No money, of course. Father lost it all to Stamford. Man showed more decency than one might have expected in marrying the eldest daughter. Only thing to do, really. Particularly with his background. But now he's got the other two sisters to provide for. Can't think they'll have anything in the way of a dowry."

"Pretty enough, the two of them, that a man might marry a sister with or without a dowry," another added.

There was some laughter, but William barely heard it. He took a step toward Miss Barlow and her sisters. Was he the only one who noticed how pale she looked? Or the way she took a deep breath, as though trying to calm her overset nerves? Perhaps if his father and uncle had not shared her dislike of attention, if he had not seen them react in just such a way, Rivendale would not have noticed her shyness. Perhaps if he had not known how his father and uncle suffered, he would not have felt such a deep sympathy. But he did.

And so William moved toward Miss Barlow, his only thought to put her at ease. He scarcely noticed Kepley following at his elbow. It was Sir Robert who noticed the two men first, and he stared at Lord Rivendale in a way that might have warned him off, and most certainly would have been daunting, had he not been so determined to speak to Miss Barlow.

But Stamford understood what Lord Rivendale had not thought to consider. He might know Miss Barlow, but the *ton* did not know that he did. Nor would she thank him if it became known how she had made his acquaintance. After all, if she wished the *ton* to know of her writing she would not be publishing as an anonymous lady of quality.

"Lord Rivendale, how good to see you again!" Stamford said, stepping between his wife and her sisters and the man.

"And you, Thomas Kepley. Have you met my wife, Lady Stamford? And may I present her sisters, Miss Theresa Barlow and Miss Elizabeth Barlow? Ladies, Lord Kepley and Lord Rivendale."

William was no fool; that hint was sufficient to warn him of the role he must play. He bowed. "Enchanted to make your acquaintance," he said to all of the ladies.

Kepley murmured something similar. They all chatted, about nothing consequential. Their conversation must have seemed unexceptionable to the interested ears of anyone who overheard them. But it was enough to establish acquaintance, so that if Miss Barlow should be seen in Lord Rivendale's company in the future, that would be considered unexceptionable as well.

Somehow Rivendale managed to find himself seated next to Miss Theresa Barlow when the musical portion of the evening began. He was not particularly surprised to discover that Kepley had managed to acquire the seat beside Miss Elizabeth Barlow. The younger sister was just as attractive as the older one and if they were anything alike, she would not see Kepley's injury as repulsive, but rather as a badge of honor for his service in the Peninsula.

The music was as dreadful as Rivendale had come to expect from this particular tone-deaf and cheap hostess. Rather than hire musicians or a singer, she had invited her friends and her daughter to display their talents. It would have been a kindness, he thought, had they all fallen prey to a grippe that stole their voices.

But for once William did not care. He was content to sit beside Miss Barlow and steal glances at her face. Even now he could not explain his fascination with her. To be sure, he admired her storytelling—and her kindness to Anna. But it was far more than that. He felt a connection to her that he could not begin to explain.

He noticed the way her hand kept stealing up to touch

the locket at her throat, and he wondered what it meant to her. It looked very old.

Others were less polite than Lord Rivendale or the Stamford party. Behind him he could hear all sorts of conversation. He tried to ignore it as thoroughly as he was ignoring the purported music. Until, that is, he felt Miss Barlow stiffen beside him, and then he did listen, wondering what it was that had caught her attention.

". . . as the first book, *The Shy Unicorn*."

"I've subscribed. They say the author is someone we know. But who?"

"Someone with children, that much is certain."

"What about Lady Fanshaw? They say that she positively dotes on her children. Shockingly so!"

"Yes, but when would she have time to write? No, it must be someone older. Perhaps a grandmother."

William cringed as he heard just such reasoning as he had gone through himself. And he wondered what they would say if they knew the author was seated right here among them. At his side he felt Miss Barlow give a choke of suppressed laughter, and he knew she must wonder very much the same thing. He risked a look at her and smiled. What he heard next, however, wiped the smile from his face.

"Isn't that Lord Rivendale?"

"First time I've seen him out and about since Lady Rivendale died."

"Hanging out for a second wife, do you think?"

"Well, it stands to reason he'll need a mother for his daughter, don't it?"

"Fixed his eyes on the Barlow chit, has he? Thinks she hasn't any other options, perhaps, and will be happy to accept any offer."

"Now, Agatha, you know very well that his fortune is indecently large."

"His wife's fortune was indecently large. But how much

of it is now his, and how much of that fortune is held in trust for the child?"

"Always wondered about his first wife's death. Mighty convenient, if you ask me. Been fighting because of his gambling debts, they say, and she threatening to refuse to pay 'em for him. And then, poof, she's dead, and he's got his hands on more funds than is good for any man."

Now William didn't dare look at the woman at his side. All he wished to do was leave and not look back. But he couldn't do it. That would only have given them cause to gossip even more. But he didn't have to like it. The question was, would it make Miss Barlow change her mind about coming to his house to help Anna?

And would Stamford still let her come? Even from where he sat, Rivendale could see the man grow more and more rigid. The rumors continued to swirl around them until the speakers grew bored with the topic of his interest in Miss Barlow and moved on to the latest *crim con* instead.

Still, William was not surprised that when the music ended and they were free to stand and circulate again, Stamford moved to his side. "Miss Barlow will not be coming to visit you at your house anymore," Stamford said in a voice pitched low enough that only Rivendale could hear.

"I understand."

Stamford went on as though William had not even spoken. "You will bring your daughter to my house to see her. There will still be gossip, but not to the degree there would be if it were the other way around."

And then Stamford moved away, taking the Barlow sisters with him. Rivendale did not try to follow. He was too stunned by Stamford's words. He understood the fellow's point of view. The trouble was, he didn't know whether it was going to be possible to get Anna into a carriage.

For the past year, anytime anyone tried to take her near a horse, she started to kick and scream. They had had to give

her laudanum to bring her to London, and since that time
William had given up trying to take her anywhere. Instead,
he had become accustomed to arranging for doctors, dress-
makers, and others to come to the house when they were
needed.

Well, he would have to see. Perhaps for Miss Barlow,
Anna would be able to overcome her fear. And if she did
not, Rivendale would plead his case with Stamford and
hope the man would relent.

So caught up was he in his own thoughts that Rivendale
did not notice Kepley until he spoke. "What the devil was
that about? Stamford looked quite grim when he spoke to
you just now. Warning you away, was he?"

William tried to smile, more for the benefit of anyone
watching than for Kepley. "Just precautions," he said, keeping his voice pitched low. "Wants to protect Miss Barlow's
reputation and I cannot say I blame him."

Kepley was silent a moment. "Miss Theresa Barlow is a
pretty young lady," he said, "and rather out of the common
way. Do you fancy her, then?"

William looked at his friend. "Don't be absurd. That
would be pure folly!"

Kepley merely smiled.

Chapter 4

Anna glowered at her father. She folded her arms across her chest, refusing to allow him to put on her pelisse.

"Very well," Lord Rivendale told her. "It's warm outside today. You can go without a pelisse."

She shook her head.

"I have explained to you that Miss Barlow cannot come here. If you wish to see her, you will have to come with me," William said.

Anna shook her head again.

Rivendale sighed and handed the offending pelisse to Nanny. He crouched down until he was at eye level with his daughter. "Very well," he said. "Stay home. I am going to see Miss Barlow. I shall give her your regrets."

And then, to keep himself from speaking frustration aloud, Lord Rivendale rose to his feet. He headed out the door that a sympathetic footman held open for him and was about to enter the carriage when Anna came running down the steps. She gave the horses a wide berth, but she flung herself into her father's arms.

There were tears in her eyes, but she had come to him, and William did not hesitate. He lifted his daughter into the carriage, signaled to the coachman, and then hastily entered the coach himself.

"I am very proud of you," he said to Anna.

His daughter's only response was to tilt up her chin and look away from him. Well, that was perfectly acceptable to

Rivendale. She could ignore him all she pleased. He was too relieved that she had overcome her fear enough to come with him to care if she gave him the cut direct.

Tessa smoothed down the dark green fabric of her skirts for what must have been the tenth time in as many minutes. Beside her, on the table, was the manuscript of a story she was working on. Anna and her father would be the first to hear what she had written of it. Would they like this story? She hoped so. But it was so difficult for Tessa to gauge the quality of her own work. Suddenly it seemed more important than it ever had before that someone like what she had written.

Miss Winsham watched her niece, disapproval evident in her expression. "It is all foolishness," she said. "Lord Rivendale will not come faster for your pacing, Theresa. I ought to have brought my box of herbs. Then I could have brewed you some tea that would make you stop acting as though your future depended upon this visit."

In spite of herself, Tessa smiled. "You would much rather be back in your cottage in the woods than here in London, wouldn't you, Aunt Margaret?" she asked. "Then you wouldn't have to deal with men, or with the *ton*."

"I don't deal with the *ton*," Miss Winsham said with a distinct sniff. "I tolerate them."

"But you miss the woods?" Tessa persisted.

Reluctantly, it seemed, Miss Winsham nodded. "I ought to be gathering herbs and drying them," she said. "And tending to the sick. Who is taking care of them while I am here?"

Tessa came to sit beside her aunt. She took her hand. "You know very well that Sir Robert has persuaded a young surgeon to go and live in the village and take care of the sick. They will be in excellent hands until we return."

"Do you mean to return?" Miss Winsham asked crossly.

"Well, of course I do!" Tessa said, taken aback.

But the older woman only stared at her, and Tessa, when she paused to consider the matter, realized that the notion no longer held the appeal it had just a week before. She refused to acknowledge that a certain Lord Rivendale had anything to do with the matter. She tried to tell herself it was the excitement of London that she liked. The chance to see things she could not see back home, the chance to visit her publisher herself. Of course, that had been just as true a week before, and it would not have been enough to keep her here, in London, then.

Nor could Tessa deny that when Lord Rivendale and Anna were shown into the room her heart seemed to beat an extra beat. Indeed, she felt a smile grow on her face of its own accord. It was the child, she tried to tell herself; it was Anna who made her feel this way. And certainly it did feel good when Anna flung her arms around Tessa's legs and hugged her as tightly as she could.

But there was a warmth that seemed to steal into her soul when Lord Rivendale took her hand and squeezed it gratefully, a warmth that had nothing to do with the child at her feet. Tessa was too well bred, of course, to let any of these feelings show in her face or in her voice. Instead, she greeted his lordship calmly, then took Anna by the hand and led her to the couch. There she lifted the child to sit beside her and began to read her latest story aloud.

If her eyes strayed, from time to time, to Lord Rivendale, Tessa quickly forced them back to the manuscript pages she held in her lap. Before she began, she explained to Anna, "You are the first to hear this story. And it is not yet finished, so you will only be hearing a part of it. Still, you must promise me that you will not tell anyone about my story. Otherwise, no one will want or need to buy my book. Do you promise?"

The child giggled and nodded. Tessa glanced over at Lord Rivendale, and he answered as solemnly as she had spoken, "I promise as well."

Disconcerted, Tessa hastily looked back at Anna and began to read. She lost track of time, caught up in the story, and in the play of emotions on Anna's face as she listened. Tessa could not help wondering if her own face had been so open, so revealing, so full of wonder, when Mama had told her stories, so many years ago, before she became too ill to do so.

When she looked across the room at Lord Rivendale, she found him staring at her as though her face were as transparent as Anna's. And Aunt Margaret looked distinctly alarmed. Indeed, the older woman rose to her feet and turned to Rivendale, blocking his view of Tessa.

"While my niece is reading to your daughter," Miss Winsham said, "why don't you come and look at Sir Robert's collection of paintings? They are considered quite exceptional."

That Lord Rivendale was reluctant could not be missed, but his manners were too good to allow him to refuse. So he rose and bowed to Tessa. "If you will excuse me, Miss Barlow?" he said, not troubling to hide a hint of irony in his voice.

Tessa nodded, not trusting herself to speak. She watched as Aunt Margaret and Lord Rivendale left the room. Only when the door was closed again behind them did she turn back to Anna, concerned that the child might be frightened that her father had left her behind. But the little girl only smiled up at Tessa trustingly and tugged at the papers on her lap, silently urging her to continue to read.

With a voice that was not altogether steady, Tessa did so.

In the hallway, Lord Rivendale regarded Miss Winsham with some amusement. That she regarded herself as guardian to Miss Barlow was unmistakable. That she thought she could succeed amused him greatly, but also touched him. He was glad that Miss Barlow had someone watching out for her.

And he liked Miss Winsham. She reminded him of his great-aunt, Phillipa. Rivendale must have spoken aloud, for she turned and looked at him.

"I am not like anyone!" she said, and dared him to contradict her.

He bowed. "I did not say you were. You are clearly an original. What I meant was that my great-aunt Phillipa is just such a determined woman. Determined to protect the entire family and accustomed to having her way. Am I wrong in thinking you are the same?"

To his surprise, Miss Winsham did not answer at once. Instead she toyed with the fringe on her shawl, and when she did answer it was to say, "I have not always had my way. But yes, you are quite correct that I stand as some sort of protector to my nieces. And that is something you had best remember. I will not allow anyone to hurt any of them!"

"I have the greatest respect for Miss Barlow," William said, his voice serious and honest.

She nodded, perhaps not entirely satisfied but willing to accept his answer, at least for the moment. She cleared her throat and returned to talking about Sir Robert's paintings, as though the conversation about her niece had never even taken place.

And if, in between, she skillfully managed to ask Lord Rivendale about the worst of the rumors concerning his marriage and his wife's death, well, he could not hold it against her. As before, his response was to be glad someone was watching out for Miss Barlow. Nor was he sorry to have the chance to deny the lies Juliet had spread about him before she died.

When they returned to the parlor, it was as if Miss Winsham had done a complete reversal of her previous opinions. She had not said so to William, but she must have been satisfied with what he told her. The moment they entered the room and saw that Miss Barlow had finished reading her story to Anna, Miss Winsham said, "Theresa, why don't you show Lord Rivendale the garden out back? I shall be happy to entertain Anna."

When she hesitated, Miss Winsham added tartly, "I may be all but in my dotage, but I still remember a few games that might amuse the child. And I have been known to tell a story or two as well."

Miss Barlow looked to him for direction, and Rivendale found himself wanting to reassure her.

"I am certain Anna will be quite happy here with your aunt," he said gently. "And I should indeed like to see the garden behind the house. If it is in any way comparable to Sir Robert's collection of paintings, then it must be well worth a turn or two."

Miss Barlow looked at him wryly, but nodded and led the way, patently not trusting herself to speak. But William saw the darkling look she gave her aunt as she passed her. As for Anna, she seemed to have no fear of staying with Miss Winsham. And that was something of a miracle in itself, for Anna was a very timid child. He could count on the fingers of one hand how many people she had heretofore trusted, as she seemed to trust both these ladies.

Still, Rivendale did not object. He meekly followed Miss Barlow out of the parlor and down the back stairs to the door that led out back. There he came to an abrupt halt as he saw what looked to him like nothing more than a tangle of brush and grass.

"This is the garden?" he could not help but ask.

Miss Barlow laughed. "Now you know why I was so astonished that Aunt Margaret should suggest I show it to you. Sir Robert is an admirable man, but he never saw the need to waste his blunt, as he put it, on something no one but himself would ever see. And my sister has not yet had time to take this garden in hand and see to its renovation."

Rivendale grinned as well. "I am not complaining," he

said. "Though I am a trifle surprised that she sent me out here with you."

A grim expression crossed Miss Barlow's face. "She is matchmaking. That is the only explanation I can credit. Which is the most inexplicable thing of all! She hates men. Or, at any rate, she has never had a good word to say, that I ever heard, about any of them. Except for my sister's husband, Sir Robert. And she was even wary of him at first."

"Is that why you never married?" William asked. "Because she would have disapproved?"

Miss Barlow looked startled, then incredulous, and finally mutinous. "Had we wished to marry, my younger sister and I, and had we found suitable partners, we would have done so—regardless of what Aunt Margaret thought."

"But you had a Season. I am certain you did. I was already married by then, but I recall you appeared to have a great many suitors."

She turned away so swiftly that he wondered if he had imagined the look of intense sadness in her face. But the very way she held herself betrayed the same emotion.

"Miss Barlow?" he asked hesitantly.

Over her shoulder, not willing to turn around, she answered him. "You are right, I did have a Season in London. And I had suitors. Too many of them. Papa would have sold me to the highest bidder had I not absolutely refused and done my best to discourage every one of them. If the example of my parents' marriage had not already discouraged me from the notion, that Season would have destroyed any illusions I might have had that it was a circumstance I envied. No, Lord Rivendale, I do not plan ever to marry."

Shocked, William was moved to protest. "Not all marriages are unhappy!"

"No?" She turned to face him, and he could see she honestly wanted to know. "My sister seems happy with Sir Robert, but it is early days for them as yet. How can I know if it will last? And what about your marriage? Was it a

happy one? I did not think so from the gossip I overheard
the other evening. Or were those lies?"

Rivendale hesitated, but in the end he could only be honest. "You overheard a great many lies the other evening.
But no, my wife and I were not happy. We each misjudged
the other, I think. But that does not mean it is always so.
My own parents were very happy with one another."

"My felicitations to them!" Miss Barlow said, not hiding
her bitterness. "They are quite the exception, then, from
everything I have heard."

William wanted to protest, to argue, but he could not.
The same thought had come to him far too often during the
years of his own marriage. He had thought himself wise to
marry for love. He had found himself miserable instead.

Fortunately, before he had to try to form a suitable reply,
Miss Barlow said, "We had best go back inside. Anna will
wonder what has happened to you."

And so the moment was lost. Rivendale did not know
whether to regret it or be glad. To speak of his marriage
with anyone was all but intolerable to him. And yet, there
were moments when he wished he could.

Inside, William gathered up his smiling daughter. He
arranged to bring Anna to visit Miss Barlow again in one
week and said all that was proper. Then he departed, not
wishing to overstay his welcome. This time, to his astonishment, Anna did not object to going outside and into the carriage. Had the day accomplished nothing else, he was
grateful for that precious favor.

He was conscious, as he lifted Anna into the carriage,
that there was a face in the parlor window above him.
William could only hope it was Miss Barlow's and not her
aunt's. He understood her disillusionment about marriage,
but for reasons he did not wish to explore, it had suddenly
become important to his peace of mind to help her understand that such pessimism was not always appropriate.

The fact that Miss Barlow might be watching him

seemed a good sign and lifted his spirits unaccountably. She could, of course, have only been interested in Anna, but that was a possibility he chose not to believe. He directed the coachman to drive to a florist first, before taking them home. Miss Barlow, he decided, deserved a posy as thanks for the time she had taken with Anna. Anna seemed delighted to agree.

Chapter 5

Miss Winsham set a brisk pace. "Do not dawdle, Theresa," she said sharply. "You insisted upon coming with me, so move along!"

Tessa said nothing. She and her sisters had talked over what to do about Aunt Margaret, and she had been the one chosen to intervene. Or, rather, at least to find out what was going on so that they would know if they should intervene.

It had been bad enough, back home, before they knew that Margaret was their aunt. Then she had simply been the woman healer who lived in a cottage in the woods, rescued children, and was suspected of being a witch. Not that there were any woods in London, but there were children, and every day Margaret disappeared, often for hours at a time.

So Alex, Tessa, and Lisbeth had decided that someone ought to find out where Aunt Margaret went. Tessa had been the one unfortunate enough to draw the short straw. Her sisters had been positively delighted.

She had not meant for Margaret to notice her, but of course she had. And insisted that Tessa join her, rather than skulking in the shadows, as she put it. So here she was, hurrying to keep up with her aunt and hoping the older woman would do what she normally did so they would not have to repeat this horrible morning.

As if she could read Tessa's mind, Miss Winsham suddenly halted, almost causing the younger woman to collide with her. "We are here," Miss Winsham said, her voice arctic with disapproval. "I do trust, Theresa, that you will not embarrass me. You are not to speak, unless spoken to first. Nor are you to question what I am doing, the choices I am making. If you cannot abide by these rules, you may as well go home right this minute!"

"Yes, Aunt Margaret."

"Hmmmph! As if I were likely to believe such patently false humility!"

Tessa did not even try to protest. What, after all, could she say? Aunt Margaret was perfectly correct. Still, she did mean to try to keep herself quiet. She presumed she would learn far more about what was going on if she did, rather than if she were to raise a fuss over her aunt's latest start.

At any rate, Miss Winsham seemed satisfied with whatever it was she saw in her niece's face, for she nodded briskly, then turned, mounted the steps, and rapped on the front door of the house before them.

The woman who opened the door was dressed very plainly. Without a word she showed Miss Winsham and her niece into a small, simply furnished parlor. There were already several people there. All of them were also dressed very plainly, so much so that Tessa was glad she had worn her oldest, plainest gown.

She sat quietly in a corner and listened. There was no doubt in her mind that it was a mistake for her to be here. It was also clear, from the suspicious looks directed her way, that the others agreed. Yet how else was she to know what was going on? And there was a great deal going on, for these were all people like Aunt Margaret.

Not everyone was involved in rescuing children, of course, though many were. Some were part of a society that wished to abolish slavery. To be sure, it was already outlawed in England, but they wished to extend that ban to the former colonies in America and to that end met here to discuss strategy and raise funds to send to their colleagues overseas.

Still, Tessa heard enough to alarm her greatly. Each person here was willing to break the law, if they believed it to be an unjust one. As Aunt Margaret had done rescuing children back home. Indeed, Tessa applauded the work these people meant to do, but she was not blind to the risks they incurred. And she worried.

When they finally left, Miss Winsham set off at a brisk pace, leaving Tessa to follow as best she could. Over her shoulder, she said to her niece, "There. Now you know, Theresa, what I have been doing. I trust you have no cause for complaint?"

"Not complaint, precisely," Tessa agreed. "It is concern I feel."

Miss Winsham paused and turned to face her niece. "I trust," she said in an austere voice, "that you are not going to be so foolish as to object to what I do?"

Tessa smiled. "How can I, when I share your concern for children? But I wonder if you are as careful as you might be, Aunt Margaret."

"I am as careful as I can be and still do what needs to be done," Miss Winsham retorted tartly.

"Yes, Aunt Margaret."

"You don't believe me, but I *am* careful. And now that you have seen, you may run along home."

Tessa started to agree, but something warned her otherwise. Perhaps it was the very slight tension in Margaret's shoulders. Perhaps it was the sudden realization that Margaret was holding her breath. In any event, Tessa straightened her shoulders and looked directly at her aunt.

"You are still hiding something!" she said in an accusing tone of voice.

"Well, of course I am!" Miss Winsham retorted indignantly. "Did you think I would tamely tell you everything? Well, I won't. I have a right to my secrets. Particularly since the less you know, the better."

"Aunt Margaret—"

Tessa tried to argue, she really did. But it was pointless. Miss Winsham had made up her mind, and nothing was going to sway her.

"Go home. I know what I am doing and I am not about to allow any of my nieces to get involved. Perhaps when you are older, but not yet!"

Before Tessa could object further, Aunt Margaret had summoned a hackney and was giving the driver the direction of Sir Robert's town house. Tessa's last sight of the older woman was to see Miss Winsham summoning a second hackney, to which, Tessa was certain, she intended to give very different directions indeed.

Tessa ought to have gone straight home. Certainly that was what she meant to do. But halfway there she was caught up in a spirit of defiance and rapped on the roof of the carriage with a cane that a previous passenger must have left behind.

The hackney driver halted the carriage and came around to ask what the problem was. When he heard that she wished to be set down right there, he hesitated, but in the end was persuaded by the fact that Tessa was willing to pay him the full amount she would have paid had she let him drive her all the way to Stamford's town house. Still, he had a worried frown on his face as he helped her down.

"Are you certain you wish to walk, miss?" he asked dubiously. "It's some ways to go."

"I am quite certain," Tessa replied as she paid the fare.

She didn't care how far she might have to walk. She felt as if she could not take being boxed in in that hackney one moment longer.

The hackney driver shrugged and climbed back onto his box. It wasn't his place to tell this young lady what she ought to do. Besides, every moment spent jawing with her was a moment lost when he could be driving a paying customer somewhere.

Tessa began to walk, trying to puzzle out what she ought to do about this matter. If she told Alex and Lisbeth, they would either join Aunt Margaret in her activities or try to stop her. Neither attempt was likely to meet with success.

She tried to put her finger on what it was that had disturbed her most about what she had seen and overheard. It wasn't as if anything overt had been said. It was more a feeling that Tessa had.

So absorbed in her thoughts was she that Tessa never saw the gentleman until she bumped into him. He recoiled in anger and immediately began to berate her.

"Look out! You ought to be more careful and watch out for your betters!"

"Betters?"

Tessa didn't realize she had said the word aloud until the man grabbed her arm. His face had turned almost purple and he said, shaking her, "Yes, your betters! What? Do you think yourself as good as your master and mistress? Have you no sense of your place?"

Abruptly Tessa realized the gentleman had mistaken her for a servant. It was her own fault, she thought, for wearing one of her older gowns. But she had done so in imitation of Aunt Margaret, who always did so on the days she went out alone. And what was she to do now?

She drew herself up to stare him down, as she had seen her aunt do upon occasion to both gentlemen and ladies who had mistaken her importance. But she had no chance to speak, for another voice intruded. An unexpectedly familiar voice it was, too.

"Let her go, Tipperton!" Lord Rivendale's voice drawled. "Need you bully servants now?"

"She was impertinent!"

"So?" Rivendale sounded amused. "Is your dignity so fragile it cannot withstand the impertinence of one maid? I had thought nothing could shake it."

The gentleman holding Tessa let go of her arm and

stepped back. He cleared his throat. "Er, of course not! Quite right, Rivendale. You, miss, off to your place of employment, right this instant!"

Tessa tried to comply, she really did. The last thing she wished for was for this stranger to realize who she was. It was the sort of *on-dit* that would be all over London in a day. Nor did she wish to have Lord Rivendale realize whose humiliation he had just witnessed. So she tried to slip past both gentlemen and hurry on her way home.

But as she passed Rivendale, she heard him draw in his breath in surprise. Tessa kept going, hoping he would decide that he was mistaken. And she prayed that, if not, he would have too much discretion to accost her in the street.

She was right. He did not accost her, at least not right away. But she was very conscious of his footsteps following hers. She had the impulse to take to her heels and try to outdistance him. After all, she and her sisters had often raced across the fields back home.

But that would have caused people to take far more notice of her than anything he could do. So she merely walked at a brisk pace and hoped he would lose interest before she reached Sir Robert's town house.

Lord Rivendale did run out of patience, but instead of abandoning his pursuit of Tessa, he took several rapid steps until he was walking side by side with her. Casually, he said, "It is not wise, Miss Barlow, for a lady to walk the streets like this. You are likely to be subjected to unpleasantness, such as just occurred with Lord Tipperton. I hope you will let me accompany you the rest of the way home."

She ought to refuse, she told herself. He had already been more than kind, and she ought not to presume on that kindness any further. But instead of refusing, Tessa found herself saying, "I should be grateful for your company—as I was grateful for your intervention just a few moments ago."

"I was glad to be of service," he said, his voice low and earnest.

Tessa waited for the questions, but they didn't come. And she was even more grateful than before, for she knew Lord Rivendale must have a great many. She didn't quite know what to do with this gentleman who had such consideration for her feelings. Indeed, he had shown consideration for the feelings of a person he thought to be an unknown servant. And it warmed her heart to think there were such men in the world. Had it been her father, Tessa knew he would have joined Tipperton in berating her.

She liked Lord Rivendale even more when he began to talk lightly of London, as though there was nothing odd about her behavior or her appearance. His brief words upon the subject appeared to be all he meant to say about the matter. And it seemed natural to invite him in when they reached Sir Robert's town house. It was a pity her sisters had to be there and so interested in her guest.

Lord Rivendale wondered what had possessed him to walk Miss Barlow home. From the moment he had realized who the poor woman was that Lord Tipperton had accosted, he should have stepped back. All right, yes, perhaps he could not simply have walked away, but what would have been so terrible about simply following her and making certain she got home safely? Why had he had to catch up with her and engage her in conversation? It could only place both of them in an awkward position.

No one had seen Rivendale with a woman since Juliet's death. If any of his acquaintances happened to see him with Miss Barlow or, worse, see him enter this house with her, the gossip would be all over London before nightfall! It would cause speculation that could only distress both Miss Barlow and him. So why had he done it? His only interest, after all, was in the way she might be able to help Anna. Wasn't it?

Because that was a question Lord Rivendale suddenly realized he did not wish to answer, did not even wish to consider, he immediately turned his attention to Miss Barlow's sisters and began to engage them in an animated, but rather pointless conversation.

By the time he escaped, half an hour later, he felt an utter fool. And the fact that he heard Miss Barlow whisper to her sisters that he had rescued her only lent speed to his footsteps! The last thing in the world he wished was for her to suddenly see him as a hero. That, after all, was what Juliet had called him—her hero. At least she had done so *before* the wedding. He could not repeat the names she had called him afterward.

And yet, for all that he fled from the word, William could not deny that in a tiny corner of his heart, he felt a hint of joy that Miss Barlow had seen him that way today.

Chapter 6

Tessa handed Mr. Plimpton her latest manuscript. This was the third book he would bring out for her. The previous two had been very successful.

"Just a little fighting," he urged. "Or maybe some nice gossip. Use some of the people you've met since you came to London. That's what sells these days."

"My books are for children. And I thought they were already successful," Tessa argued.

Mr. Plimpton looked away. "Well, yes, but they could sell more copies. A lot more copies. You don't have to libel anyone, really. Just make a few of the characters recognizable. We'd have all London reading, hoping to discover someone they knew in the story."

Tessa shook her head. "No. I won't do it. And if you dislike the stories I write, then I shall be happy to take them elsewhere."

"Here, no, don't do that!" Mr. Plimpton said, with some alarm.

"Then I may continue to write the stories as I wish?" Tessa asked.

He grumbled, but in the end agreed. The young lady was already his best-selling author. "Mind you think about it, though," he said. "Just think about it."

"I shall, but I cannot think I will change my mind."

"Yes, yes, just give me the manuscript."

Tessa did so, and then happily left the offices of her publisher. Outside she shook her head in disbelief. Was the man mad? Did he really not feel content with the success they had had? It seemed remarkably foolish to her, and she was glad she had refused his pressure to do as he said. It was fortunate for her peace of mind that she did not know what went on in the office after she was gone.

"Well?" the thin young man asked Mr. Plimpton.

The publisher snorted. "She won't do it. Says she don't see the need."

"Let me fix it up," the young man urged. "I can add the parts we need. Just a description, here and there, ought to do it. Don't matter if it fits or not. So much the better if they think it's a bit of slander. They'll be eager to buy up all the copies."

Mr. Plimpton hesitated. But he was a greedy man. As much as the previous volumes had brought in, he wished for even more profit, and this seemed such an easy way to get it. So now he nodded. "All right. But mind, do it carefully. Just a hint here and there in the descriptions. We don't want to be shut down. We'll deny everything and let them wonder. You get to work on this," he said, handing the manuscript over to the young man, "and I'll get to work on the note to be delivered to Fleet Street. I know a scribbler or two would be happy to hear something good for a gossip column."

Lord Rivendale stared at his daughter, and at Nanny. The older woman stood, arms crossed over her chest, tapping her foot. "I can't do a thing with her, sir, and it's time and past she had a governess who could! Now she won't eat without it being them pastries Cook made when that lady came and read to her. And she wants to wear just them dresses she wore them days you took her to see the lady, or the lady came here. She won't do no lessons, just pretends to scribble on paper as if she were writing down stories of her own!"

William suppressed a sigh of exasperation. He was not meant to be a father, he thought—at least not to a child without a mother. Why the devil couldn't he simply reason with her? Why did Anna have to be so stubborn?

And yet, in a way, he understood, he really did. He, too, wished he could spend more time with Miss Barlow. He just wished he knew what to do with his daughter. He would not have had the patience Nanny had if Anna had tried such tricks with him.

He knelt beside his daughter, and when she would not look at him, he took away the paper from her. Instantly his placid daughter turned into a termagant. She reached for the paper, arms flailing, and actually struck her father in the face by accident.

Rivendale easily captured her wrists with one hand. And then he forced her to look at him. "If you wish this back," he said carefully but firmly, "if you wish to have paper and pen at all, you must listen to Nanny. You must eat as she tells you to eat, and dress as she tells you to dress. And for each sheet of paper you have for this purpose, you must do a little of your lessons with her."

Anna stared back, her lower lip trembling, and a mutinous look in her eyes.

"I mean it," Rivendale told her sternly. "You are to do as Nanny says. Or no more paper and ink. Promise?"

For a long moment, a very long moment, matters hung in the balance. Then Anna slowly nodded, even as a tear trickled down her cheek. Gently William wiped it away.

"I know, sweetling," he said in his softest, most gentle voice. "You miss her. You wish you could see her every day. That's not possible, I'm afraid. But you will see her this week. Think how proud of you she would be if I could tell her that you did your lessons with Nanny."

Again the mutinous look came into his daughter's eyes. Still, Rivendale pressed the point.

"Miss Barlow must value lessons. She must have liked them when she was young. Otherwise she could not have become the wonderful storyteller she is. She had to learn to write her letters neatly, or no publisher would have taken her stories and put them into books. So she would want you to pay attention to your lessons as well."

It was not, perhaps, a complete surrender, for William could still see rebellion in his daughter's face. But she did turn and sit back down at the table and look to Nanny for direction. The woman shot a grateful look at Lord Rivendale and let out a sigh of relief of her own. But at least, he thought, her voice was more gentle as she began to talk to Anna again.

Once he was certain Anna and Nanny were deep into his daughter's lessons, William slipped out of the nursery and down the stairs toward the library. He had some letters to answer and invitations to peruse. Now that he had gone to one social event, the *ton* seemed to have recalled his existence. Every hostess, it seemed, wanted to have Lord Rivendale grace her event—and there were a surprising number of events, given that it was not even the Season right now.

But William did not make it to his library. To be sure, he had his hand on the door and the door halfway open, but then Giles, his majordomo, appeared and said, "Lady Rivendale is below, sir. She just arrived."

William understood his majordomo's air of dismay, for he shared it. He adored his mother, but there was no denying that every time she came to town, she tried to turn his life and his household upside down!

"I shall be there straightaway," he promised.

The moment Giles left, Rivendale rested his forehead, eyes closed, against the library door. His mother! It only

wanted that. Still, there was no point putting it off. He had
best go and greet her.

She was, as he expected, still in the foyer. He had not
bothered to tell Giles to show her to the parlor or drawing
room because he had known she would refuse until every
piece of her luggage was out of the hallway, and she had
finished quizzing each of his servants as to the events of
their lives and his own since her last visit.

"Mother! What a delightful surprise!" he said, descend-
ing the last few steps to where she stood.

Lady Rivendale whirled to face William, a smile spreading across her face. "My dearest son!" she exclaimed.
"How are you? How is Anna?"

She flung herself at him, and dutifully William embraced
the petite, silk-clad figure who had given birth to him.
From the tips of her delicately dressed toes to the top of her
improbably radiant hair, Lady Rivendale was a beauty. She
smiled up at him, and he could not help but smile back.

"What are you doing here, Mother?" he asked.

She waved a hand, and avoided meeting his eyes. "You
know I always come to London at some point to refresh my
wardrobe. My gowns are sadly out of style."

As his mother had never in her life worn anything the
least bit dowdy or out of fashion, and the violet silk she
wore right now would have done credit to any lady in London, this was patently untrue. But William did not contradict her. Instead he asked, "How long do you mean to
stay?"

Again she smiled, disarmingly, up at him. "Why? Are
you already impatient to have me gone? I warn you that I
have been bored, positively bored, in the countryside, and
need the excitement of London to revive me!"

As Rivendale was well aware that his mother's days back
home were filled with good works and looking after his
tenants, whether they wished for her care or not, he doubted
very much she was ever bored. The *ton* might look at his

mother and see what some had called a will-o'-the-wisp or butterfly, but William knew the serious heart beneath the giddy exterior. He knew the fine mind hidden behind the laughing smile—even if she rarely chose to admit to it.

"I see," he told her. "And you have no other purpose than that? Very well, I am delighted to see you, and Anna will be as well. She is upstairs in the nursery. Nanny would not thank us for interrupting the lesson she has finally been able to begin with Anna. But you may see her later."

Now Lady Rivendale frowned. "You still have not found a governess to take Anna in charge?"

William flushed. "What governess would take on a child who does not speak?" he asked irritably. "Besides, Anna has taken every one I brought to meet her in dislike at first sight—and so have I."

His mother nodded. "Yes, that would make matters difficult. Very well, I shall undertake to find you a governess for Anna while I am here."

It was his turn to grin. "I ought to object to such high-handedness," he told her with a chuckle, "but I am far too grateful. If you can find a governess for Anna, one my daughter will accept, I shall be delighted."

Lady Rivendale merely smiled in return, serenely confident of her ability to accomplish whatever she wished. It was from her that William had learned to do so himself—until his wife's death and Anna's silence. None of his skills, none of his intelligence, none of anything that life or his mother or his father had taught him, had been enough to persuade his daughter to speak.

Rivendale took his mother's hand and tucked it into his elbow. "Come," he said. "My housekeeper has no doubt brewed a pot of tea and filled a plate with pastries. At any moment she will be bringing it to the drawing room for you. For you are a prime favorite with her, you know. So why don't we go up to the drawing room? Once we are comfortable, you can tell me about the estate, and about your journey, and whatever else you think I ought to know."

As a tactic to deflect, or at least delay, her questions, it was effective. William had no illusions that he would escape his mother's inquisition unscathed, but he would put the matter off as long as he could. For reasons he could not explain, he found himself most reluctant to tell her about Miss Barlow, and what else that was new in his life would she consider important?

"Your uncle," Lady Rivendale said when they were in the drawing room, and she had poured the tea that the housekeeper had indeed brought in to them, "has had another of his odd starts. This time he is writing naturalists and asking them about a theory he has concerning some creatures found in the far eastern islands. He has not been out of his library for more than a few minutes at a time for weeks. Fortunately, the bailiff, and everyone else, know what they are to do—even without his directions. I do not know what possessed your father to appoint him your guardian! Or why you kept him on, after you came of age."

"Because he was Papa's favorite brother, of course," William said lightly. "And I keep him on because where else is he to go? Besides, someone must look after things."

"You could come back home and do so yourself," Lady Rivendale said gently.

Instantly William was on his feet, his back to his mother. "No! I will not go back there! You know very well why. I will not subject myself, or Anna, to the memories. Good God, Mama! Anna has not spoken in a year. Do you truly wish me to risk what little progress we have made by taking her back to where it all began?"

"It might do her good. I understand some of the experts you have consulted have even said as much," Lady Rivendale countered gently.

He did not bother to ask where her information came

from. He knew her too well to even be surprised. Instead he merely shrugged. "I will not come back to the estate."

"The estate needs a steady hand—your hand," Lady Rivendale persisted.

Over his shoulder, William said carelessly, "Let my uncle do the best he can. Even if the place were to go to rack and ruin, I would not care."

"Some day your son may care."

Rivendale turned to face his mother. "I will never have a son," he said, his face cold and grim, his voice the same. "I will never have another child, not even for the sake of begetting an heir. I have told you so before—you simply choose to refuse to believe me. But it is the truth. Let the estate and title go to whom it will."

His mother sighed. She knew better to argue. Still, she did not—could not—hide her dismay, and that touched William in a way that no amount of arguing could have done. Swiftly he sat beside her again and took her hand in his.

"Tell me about my uncle," he said coaxingly. "How is his health these days? Has he recovered from that winter cough he had?"

Lady Rivendale tried to smile, tried to speak in a rallying tone. "Yes, he has. Mind you, I worry that he locks himself away in the library so much. I tell him he ought to get out and walk more, but he does not wish to hear it. He eats stintingly, as always when caught up in a project. Otherwise he is in excellent state."

She paused and then spoke with a carelessness that fooled neither of them. "And you, William? How are you, and how have you been filling your days?"

"I am also in excellent state," he replied, with a matching air of carelessness that did not fool his mother either. "Doing this and that. But what about the vicar back home? I had heard there was some sort of scandal?"

His mother wished to press him with questions, that

much was unmistakable to William, who knew her so well. But she could not resist telling him about the vicar, either. After all, a scandal in an obscure parish that was sufficiently outrageous to reach London was something few people could resist talking about, and his mother most certainly was not one of those few.

If Lady Rivendale disliked such tactics, she did not say so. Instead she merely watched him with distressingly shrewd eyes. And smiled each time he turned the subject to yet another *crim con* or *on-dit* or a question about matters back home. Eventually, however, even William ran out of things to say. And that was when his mother leaned forward to pounce.

"Tell me everything you know about this Miss Barlow I have been hearing so much about," she said.

William hesitated. He had promised to keep Miss Barlow's secret about her writing. But did that include his mother? The rest of the *ton* assumed, of course, that he had an unaccountable *tendre* for the woman, but how could he risk letting his mother think so as well? There was no telling what she might decide to do, if she thought it in his best interests for her to meddle. And she had, for some time now, been hinting that he ought to look about him for a wife—one who could be a mother to poor Anna.

In the end he simply looked at her and said, "Why don't you come and meet her yourself? Anna and I are to go and see her tomorrow morning."

"Anna?" Lady Rivendale leaned back and blinked at her son. "You take Anna with you when you go to call upon her? I had heard it was so, but that seemed so foolish I discounted the thought."

A smile played about William's lips as he answered, "Come and see for yourself, Mother."

Lady Rivendale drew in a deep breath. "Well, it is an unconventional manner in which to conduct a courtship, but then neither you nor your father has ever been a conventional man. And if Miss Barlow does not object to you bringing your daughter, why, then, I must suppose she will not greatly object to my presence either."

"She will like you very well," William predicted. "And I suspect you will like her."

Lady Rivendale lowered her eyes, clearly trying to conceal her thoughts from her son. "Mmmmm," she said. "We shall see. We shall see."

Chapter 7

L ord Rivendale had no chance to warn Tessa. Nor did she have any reason to think this morning would be any different than any of the other mornings when he brought his daughter to see her.

"You had best stop pacing, or you will wear straight through Sir Robert's fine carpet, and then what will you say to him?" Miss Winsham warned her niece sternly.

Tessa turned and smiled at her aunt. "I shall tell him it was Lord Rivendale's fault for being late. I am persuaded Sir Robert would quite understand."

"Hmmmph. That's neither here nor there," Miss Winsham persisted. "You ought not to appear so eager. It does not become a lady. You ought to make the gentleman think you are doing him a favor to allow his company."

"It is Lord Rivendale's daughter I am eager to see," Tessa replied, tilting up her chin.

"Oh, to be sure," her aunt said, not troubling to hide her disbelief. "Such a delightful child, isn't she? Quite the thing to put a blush in your cheeks. No doubt she is the reason you are wearing your most becoming gown? And naturally you would be pacing back and forth with impatience at the thought of seeing her!"

Before Tessa had to answer, their visitors were announced. "Lord Rivendale, Lady Rivendale, Miss Rivendale," Wilkins intoned, his voice expressionless, though his eyes betrayed his avid curiosity.

Tessa somehow managed to greet Lord Rivendale and his daughter, as she always did, and to welcome Lady Rivendale, even though her mind was filled with questions. Questions that Rivendale was kind enough to answer, though naturally they had not been spoken aloud.

"My mother has come to visit me," he said, handing Lady Rivendale to a seat. "She needs, she says, to improve her wardrobe. As though she would not look dashing and beautiful in anything she wore!"

Tessa smiled at that, and at the warm affection evident between mother and son.

"You must tell us the direction of your dressmaker, if you will," Miss Winsham told Lady Rivendale. "For our own wardrobes are sadly in need of replenishing, and I have yet to see anything so flattering or fetching as what you are wearing since we arrived in London."

Tessa blushed at her aunt's forwardness, but Lady Rivendale seemed more than willing to oblige, even going so far as to offer to accompany the ladies on any day they chose.

"You are very kind," Tessa said, in a faint voice, thinking of their limited funds and how unlikely it was that they could afford whomever Lady Rivendale chose to patronize. She tried to find a polite way to refuse. "But we should not wish to put you to any trouble."

"Oh, it would be no trouble," Lady Rivendale said airily. "I should very much enjoy such an expedition!"

Perhaps Lord Rivendale noticed Tessa's discomfort, for he hastened to intervene. "Yes, well, in any event," he said, "my mother heard we were coming to see you, and she asked to come as well."

Tessa hesitated, uncertain how to respond to such a statement. How much had Lord Rivendale told his mother? To what purpose had she asked to come? She could ask neither of these questions aloud.

But Lady Rivendale answered the second question anyway. "I wished to see what manner of young woman could hold my granddaughter so in thrall that she would willingly climb into a carriage," she said, fixing her clear blue eyes on Tessa's face. "And what manner of young woman would so willingly entertain such a child."

Anna, who had seemed to be oblivious to the conversation swirling around her as she wandered about the room, now discovered the sheaf of papers that held the latest version of Tessa's story. She grabbed it up with a grin of triumph and promptly plopped it into Tessa's lap. Then she climbed up on the sofa beside her. She looked up at Tessa with both trust and expectation in her eyes.

Lady Rivendale drew in a deep breath of surprise at the sight. Tessa looked at Lord Rivendale for help. Did his mother know? Had he betrayed her secret?

He shook his head. It was barely perceptible, but both Tessa and Lady Rivendale saw him. "I will not ask what it is that you wish to keep from me," the older woman said to both Tessa and her son, "but you will understand that the more curious I am, the more I am likely to pry to try to find out. And since I will have to ask others, they will no doubt gossip even more than they already do."

Lord Rivendale looked at Tessa. She could read a hint of desperation, a sense of helplessness in his gaze. Well, she could not blame him. She did not know how she would handle such a mother either!

It was Miss Winsham who took the matter out of their hands. "My niece writes," she said bluntly. "Stories. Children's stories. And people buy 'em. Your granddaughter likes my niece's stories. And Theresa likes reading 'em to Anna. That's the long and the short of it. And I'll thank you to keep that information to yourself. The *ton* wouldn't look kindly on that sort of eccentricity. Especially not in a girl who ain't even wed yet."

Now Lady Rivendale fixed her gaze on the other older woman. "Don't I know you?" she asked. "In school, perhaps? You were the Winsham girl. The one who was sent home for dallying with the surgeon's assistant?"

Miss Winsham sniffed. "Wondered when you would remember me. I wanted to learn how to heal, that's all. No one believed that, of course. They'd rather believe I wanted to kiss the fellow. As if anyone could be that foolish!"

Lady Rivendale nodded slowly. "I believe you. You used to help me with my work. I wasn't much of a scholar, but you were. How could I not have recognized you?"

"Nonsense! I always thought you understood as much as I did, though you didn't wish to admit it. As for why you did not recognize me, perhaps it is because I have changed over the years," Miss Winsham told her in acid tones. "And not for the better, I'll be bound."

Lady Rivendale smiled. "Oh, but you have changed for the better. I think it's that you have more presence, more self-assurance than you did back then. And that, by the by, is a good thing, in my opinion!"

As the two older women began to reminisce about their school days together, Lord Rivendale came to sit on the other side of Tessa.

In a low voice that would not disturb his mother or Miss Winsham, he said, "My deepest apologies. I would have protected you from her if I could. But, not knowing that you write, and that you have been telling stories to Anna at my request, my mother got it into her head that my interest in you was romantic. She would not be put off from coming to inspect you. I didn't know what to tell her. It is your secret, after all, about the writing."

"Or at any rate it was," Tessa said ruefully. "Aunt Margaret has put paid to any notion of keeping your mother from finding out. Can she be trusted to keep silent about it? Or will she wish to tell her friends?"

Lord Rivendale hesitated. "If she took you in dislike," he said slowly, "she might very well tell. But as she and your aunt are in a fair way to becoming fast friends again, I suspect she will do her best to keep your secret. I only hope she may not betray it in an unguarded moment. But," he added, as if he could feel her distress, "I do not think that likely. My mother may appear to have more hair than wit, Miss Barlow, but truly she has a far better mind than anyone looking at her would give her credit for—despite her words to your aunt about not being a scholar!"

"Well, at least she no longer thinks you to be dangling after me," Tessa said with a wry smile.

Lord Rivendale hesitated, and Tessa found herself wondering what it was he did not want to say. But before she could ask, even if she had found the courage to do so, Anna tugged at Tessa's arm and patted the sheaf of papers on her lap.

"You will excuse us," Tessa told Lord Rivendale, rising to her feet. "I shall take Anna into the smaller parlor and read to her there."

He nodded. For a moment Tessa thought he would ask to go with them, but in the end he did not, and she could not decide whether to feel relieved or disappointed. But Anna did not allow her time to worry over the matter. The child might not speak, but she heard and understood perfectly well, and now she tugged more urgently at Tessa's hand.

As they left the room she could hear Lord Rivendale's mother demand to know where Tessa was going with Anna. Tessa could only be grateful to escape those watchful eyes, and that someone else would have to answer her questions.

William stared into his glass of brandy. His mother's questions had not stopped, from the moment they climbed into his carriage with Anna until the moment they returned to his town house and he escaped to his library. In somewhat a sense of desperation he told his mother, "Have Anna show you the books Miss Barlow has written that sit on her shelf."

That had bought him a little time but, over dinner, the

questions began again. How the devil did he know what his intentions toward Miss Barlow might be? What did it matter, other than that she was bringing Anna out of herself, and was willing to read to the child? Nor could he see the point of his mother's questions about gossip. Both he and Miss Barlow were doing everything they could to minimize tongues wagging. He had promised to protect her secret. What more was there he ought to do?

But that was not enough for his mother, and while he sat over his brandy, she was sifting through the invitations he had received, deciding to which events she was going to have him escort her. And he could guess, with a shudder, her plans to visit all her bosom bows and trade stories about their children and grandchildren. He did not like to think what the results of those expeditions might be. Once his mother had the bit between her teeth, she was inclined to run with it, and heaven help anyone who tried to hinder or resist her plans for them. He could only hope she would find herself drawn into someone else's dilemma, and not think a moment more about his own.

With a gulp, he downed the last of the brandy, and then went in search of his mother. There was no point, after all, in putting off the inevitable.

As he expected, she was looking through the invitations. "Sir Robert does not entertain?" she asked, looking up at him as he came into the room.

Rivendale took a seat opposite his mother. "Sir Robert," he said carefully, "has achieved a measure of acceptance with his marriage to Henley's daughter. But he knows better than to press his luck by holding balls or such that others might delight to ignore."

"I see. And do the ladies, the Barlow sisters and their aunt, go out and about?" Lady Rivendale persisted.

"Sometimes," William cautiously agreed.

"Perhaps most likely to the invitations in this pile?" his mother asked, holding up the ones he had set aside.

William flushed. "Perhaps," he reluctantly agreed.

"Then, heavens above, why did you allow me to waste my time going through these others, William?" Lady Rivendale demanded.

"I thought you might wish to accept one or more of them," he replied carelessly, as though it was a matter of no importance to him.

She was not deceived. "To be sure. Nonetheless, we shall accept the ones in your pile."

William tried one more time to protect Miss Barlow from his mother's attention. "She is trying to help Anna, nothing more, Mother!"

Lady Rivendale snorted, and it was a distinctly unladylike sound, greatly at odds with her dainty appearance. "Nonsense! It is time, and past, that you were thinking of marrying again. And this time I pray you will not choose a pretty widgeon with not a thought in her head! You need a woman of sense, and so far as I can tell, Miss Barlow is just such a one."

"I doubt she would have me, even if I did entertain such an absurd possibility," William said, a hint of desperation in his voice.

"Why absurd?" Lady Rivendale demanded indignantly. "Surely she does not fancy herself too good for you?"

"It is common knowledge among the *ton* that Miss Barlow does not wish to marry," her son said in an austere voice meant to cow his mother.

"Why, then, you would just have to persuade her," Lady Rivendale replied, with wide-open, innocent-looking eyes. "I am certain you could do so, if you tried."

"But what if I don't wish to try?"

Lady Rivendale leaned forward and took her son's hand. Her voice was serious as she said, "I do not mean to tease you, William, but I watched for years as your first marriage became more and more unhappy. I saw the way Juliet went from alt to despair and back again, leading you in the devil of a dance. I would not for the world wish such unhappiness upon you again. But you know it need not be that way. Your father and I were very happy together. That is what I wish for you! Someone who shares your laughter, and holds you when you both need to cry. Someone who understands your faults, but loves your strengths. Someone who makes you better than yourself when you are with her, and who is better for it when she is with you."

Lady Rivendale paused, searching for the words to persuade her son. "You are lonely. I see it in your eyes, however much you may try to deny it. And while your first marriage may have been worse than lonely, I wish for you a companion who will share your interests and invite your trust. Someone to whom you may bare your soul. And when that day comes, you will never be lonely again."

"And you think Miss Barlow is such a one?" William asked incredulously. "A woman you have met but once? Who spent most of that time in another room reading to Anna?"

Lady Rivendale leaned back in her chair, and a smile played about her lips. "I saw how you looked at her, and how she looked at you," she said. "And, yes, based upon that short acquaintance, I think it possible Miss Barlow is the right match for you. Granted, I should like the opportunity to meet her again, and to speak with her about her wishes, her dreams, and perhaps even her hopes. But I have not seen such a promising possibility in many years. And," Lady Rivendale said as she rose to her feet, making it her parting shot, "she is nothing like Juliet!"

Then, before William could protest, his mother sailed out of the room, leaving him wishing the bottle of brandy were close to hand. He did not want to believe his mother. He did not like to think of the mistake his marriage had been. But it was impossible to get her words out of his head. Not when they echoed the thoughts he had when he woke alone in the early hours of the morning, the moments when he wondered if he was always going to be alone. Not when they echoed the hopes, the dreams he allowed himself on his brightest mornings.

Still he shuddered, hoping that Miss Barlow would never learn of the things his mother had said about her. That would be all he needed, for her to hear such fantasies and know that in his heart there were moments when he did indeed contemplate the notion of something far more than just friendship between them. From what he had seen of her, and what he had heard about the Barlow sisters, it would be enough to send her running the other way. Then what would he and Anna do?

Chapter 8

It began as a whisper, a swirl of rumor spoken just out of Tessa's hearing. Not that anyone tried to prevent her from hearing. After all, no one, other than her publisher, her family, and Lord and Lady Rivendale, had any reason to think she would care what was said. No one knew it could in any way pertain to her.

And yet, as unattached as she was in London, as few friends as she had been able to make, Tessa simply had no one to tell her about the rumors, which began first among those with children—those who would have bought her books.

That Tessa did not notice the cause of those rumors was because beyond admiring the handsome volumes on her shelf, she did not open her own books. What was the need? She had written the words and knew them already.

So it was several days before she received even a hint of the disaster facing the lady of quality who had written *The Unhappy Monster*. And it was unfortunately in Lord Rivendale's company that she heard it.

Lady Rivendale was holding a small party at her son's house, and she had been kind enough to invite Tessa's entire family. "For I am trying to persuade my son to go out and about more, and I mean for this to be a way for him to reacquaint himself with my old friends who can help him. But I should like him to have some of his friends there as well. I am also, of course, inviting Lord Kepley."

So Tessa, Lisbeth, Alex, Sir Robert, and Miss Winsham all moved about the rooms, greeting people they knew, being introduced to those they didn't. Lord Thomas Kepley and Lord Rivendale both took it upon themselves to make certain the two unmarried Barlow sisters had everything they wished. Meanwhile, Aunt Margaret settled in beside Lady Rivendale, and that was where they found her some time later.

That was also where they heard the fatal words. "Have you read the latest outrageous children's tale, *The Unhappy Monster*?" one of the guests asked.

"I believe my daughter likes all the author's books," Lord Rivendale answered austerely.

"She adores them," Lady Rivendale corrected, with a sideways glance at Tessa. "One day I must take the time to read one of them myself."

"Yes, you ought," her friend agreed. "Everyone is wondering who the authoress is, and how she had the audacity to write such things."

"What things?" Rivendale asked with a frown, looking as confused as Tessa felt.

The woman tittered. "She has disguised members of the *ton* as creatures in her stories. I vow she has offended Prinny and Lord Byron and Beau Brummell, and no doubt a good many others as well."

Tessa straightened. Lord Rivendale looked at her, lifting one brow in silent inquiry. She shook her head slightly, then turned to the woman and took a deep breath.

She was afraid her face had gone pale, and her voice was not altogether steady, but she could not help that. She tried to sound as careless as she could as she asked, "Are you certain, madam? I have read some of those books, and I recall nothing of the sort."

"Oh, I am quite certain," the woman said with smug satisfaction. "The moment I heard the rumors, I checked with my daughter's governess to see if we had the book, and we did. And I devoured it, positively devoured it!"

"You may be certain I shall have a look at my grand-daughter's bookshelf the first thing in the morning as well," Lady Rivendale said, her voice grim.

She was careful not to look at Tessa, which left the younger woman wanting to sink through the floor. It was nonsense, all nonsense! And yet something must be in the book to make people say such things. The moment she returned home, she was going to inspect her own copies of the book. But for the moment, there was nothing to be done. She could not even defend herself, for if she did, everyone would know the identity of the lady of quality. And if that had been inadvisable before, it was ten times more so now.

Miss Winsham apparently felt no such compunction. She appeared at Tessa's side and sniffed loudly. "Nonsense!" she said. "No doubt it is simply a few credulous fools with ridiculous imaginations, seeing things in harmless stories that were never meant to be there. And naturally, once the notion has been planted in everyone else's minds, they will see it as well, even if there is nothing to see."

But the woman shook her head. "Read the book," she advised. "You will not say so then."

It was Sir Robert who salvaged the situation. He yawned ostentatiously and said carelessly, "What nonsense! Who cares about a book? Now the latest story about Prinny's corsets, that is what I find amusing!"

And as everyone else did as well, it was sufficient to divert attention from *The Unhappy Monster* and its unhappy author. Lord Rivendale drew Tessa aside, into the library and shut the door behind them.

"You must not worry," he told her. "Your aunt no doubt has the right of things. Someone saw something that was not there, and no one else wishes to admit they cannot, and so the rumor spreads."

Tessa shook her head. "You may be right, but it will not help the reputation of my books. Nor my own, should anyone realize I wrote them."

Lord Rivendale came forward and stared at the locket at her throat. He outlined it with his finger. "I believe in you," he said softly.

And then he lifted her hands to his lips and kissed them. Tessa found herself close to tears, grateful for his belief in her and tugged by feelings she had never known before. When Lord Rivendale drew her closer, she did not resist. What did propriety matter when he offered comfort, a comfort she needed so dearly?

Even when his lips descended toward hers, Tessa did not draw away. Somehow it seemed this was where she had been heading since the first day she walked into his house. This was what her heart craved and she could not, would not, deny it.

The library door opened and Kepley's voice intruded. "Lord Rivendale, Miss Barlow. Lady Rivendale sent me in search of you. It seems that Stamford and his party are ready to leave. You are wanted, Miss Barlow."

Tessa turned to see Kepley standing at the doorway. She could only be grateful it was he and not some stranger. She pulled herself free and tried to compose herself as she replied, "Thank you. I am ready to leave as well."

She brushed past Kepley. Before the door closed behind her, leaving the two men in the library together, she heard Kepley say, "A tasty tidbit, but most unwise of you to dally with her in such a way. Much better, much wiser, to choose a married woman. One who will not expect the impossible of you."

But she did not expect the impossible, Tessa told herself resolutely. Lord Rivendale had merely been comforting her—surely that was all.

She found the others waiting for her. Tessa hastily took her leave of a very thoughtful-looking Lady Rivendale and of others she knew. In the carriage everyone was careful not to ask Tessa about the book. Everyone, that is, save her aunt.

"What possessed you to be so foolish?" Miss Winsham demanded.

"I wasn't," Tessa replied. "Mr. Plimpton asked me to do something of the sort, but I refused."

"Well, you had best look at the volumes he published, and see whether there is any truth to the rumors," Miss Winsham persisted.

"Is it possible you did not realize you were describing your creatures in ways that others could see as members of the *ton*?" Alex suggested.

Tessa looked at her older sister. "Perhaps," she said slowly. "That is what I fear. But I cannot know until I look at the story again."

"It will be the first thing we do when we return home," Lisbeth said. "And Stamford must read it as well. After all, he knows the persons of the *ton* far better than we do. He will be better able to recognize them—if they are there in the story."

So it was that half an hour later all three sisters, Stamford, and Aunt Margaret were ensconced in the library, copies of *The Unhappy Monster* open on their laps. It was Alex who found the first reference. Stamford found the second. Tessa read what they pointed out with a sinking sense of disbelief.

"I did not describe that creature as having red hair and brows," she protested. "Nor did I put a corset on any of my animals, and certainly not that one!"

"Someone did so," Stamford said grimly.

"Do you have the original manuscripts?" Alex asked.

Tessa shook her head. "No. I did not think it necessary to make a copy. I have my earlier versions, but they are not complete."

"With the next book you turn in, you will keep an exact

copy," Stamford said, rising to his feet and pacing about the room. "And you will show it to me before you take it to Mr. Plimpton. Then if he alters the text we shall be able to prove it."

"N-n-next book?" Tessa asked. "Am I going to write another book?"

"Oh, I think so," Stamford assured her. "You already have the story written, I believe." She nodded. "Good. I shall read it after you make a copy, and then I shall deliver it personally, along with a warning."

"I wish to speak with Mr. Plimpton myself," Tessa said firmly.

"Very well, we shall both deliver it," Stamford told her. "And Mr. Plimpton will print an apology in the front of it, for the alterations to the last one."

Tessa hoped Stamford was correct, but somehow she did not think Mr. Plimpton was a man to do anything of the sort. Still, she would do as Stamford suggested. And she would be grateful for his company when she went to deliver the manuscript. Somehow she did not wish to face the man alone.

With the assurance of Stamford's support, it was not her book that kept Tessa awake nearly until dawn. Rather it was the memory of Lord Rivendale's face, in his library, as he told her he believed in her, and as he bent forward to kiss her.

Was she a wanton to have allowed such a thing? And could it possibly mean as much to him as it had to her? Tessa wished she knew.

Had she been able to see that Lord Rivendale also found it difficult to sleep until close to dawn, it might have reassured her. But as it was, all she knew was that her heart was feeling things she had not known it could, and she was not certain whether to be glad or sorry.

Chapter 9

The next morning, Tessa realized the situation was even worse than she had considered it to be the night before. When she read *The Unhappy Monster* all the way through, she discovered that someone had described one of the other characters in such terms that no one could mistake him for anyone other than Lord Rivendale.

Tessa felt even more distressed than she had the night before. How had this been allowed to happen? Mr. Plimpton, of course. He must have decided to do what she would not agree to do. He had embellished the text in ways she would not agree to do. And so the *ton* had her books to gossip about.

Worse, with the character representing Lord Rivendale playing such a prominent role in her story, some might begin to look at his acquaintances to discover the author—and their scrutiny might settle on Tessa. It was astonishing that it had not done so last night at the party.

Worst of all, by now Lady Rivendale and Lord Rivendale must have read the book. Would they believe she had written these things after all?

It was, Tessa was forced to admit, an unmitigated disaster. The sooner she made a copy of her latest manuscript, and she and Stamford visited Mr. Plimpton, the better, she told herself. She would not, she vowed, allow him to publish any more of her stories unless he published the correct version of her book and printed an apology in the papers.

The significance of the situation lent speed to Tessa's fingers. Her sisters even helped to copy parts of the manuscript. Thus it was that a very pale but determined Tessa and a stern Stamford were able to descend upon Mr. Plimpton's offices that afternoon. Mr. Plimpton seemed delighted to see Tessa and reached eagerly for the manuscript she held in her hand. Stamford stepped between them.

"Not so quickly," Stamford warned him. "There is the little matter of a manuscript you altered without Miss Barlow's permission."

"I merely improved it a little. And the sales have gone up enormously," Mr. Plimpton protested. "All of London is now eager for your next work, Miss Barlow. Why, the number of people who have already subscribed is double the initial subscription for the last."

"I have no doubt of that," Stamford said. "But you are going to print an apology, and you will also issue volumes that accurately reflect the manuscript Miss Barlow gave you."

"I told you I would not agree to this sort of thing!" Tessa added indignantly.

Mr. Plimpton dropped the obsequious air. He moved to sit behind his desk as he steepled his hands together. "I think not, sir," he told Stamford. "I am the publisher. I have the right to make the improvements I see fit to make."

"I will not allow you to have any more of my manuscripts, if you do not issue revised editions!" Tessa exclaimed, her anger evident.

Mr. Plimpton smiled, and it was not a pleasant smile. He leaned forward and rested his elbows on the desk. "My dear Miss Barlow," he said in the nastiest of voices, "without my alterations, no one wants your manuscripts. They are nice little tales, to be sure, but the subscription they would draw on their own merits would scarcely pay for the cost of printing them up. No, either you allow the revisions I require or you find another publisher."

"I shall happily find another publisher," Tessa said through clenched teeth.

"You may not find it easy to do so. And recollect that I am not asking you to make the revisions," Mr. Plimpton pointed out lightly. "I am perfectly happy to have my nephew do so for you. Particularly as his efforts have met with such enormous success thus far."

Tessa stared at him for a long moment, then turned on her heel and stalked out of the offices. Stamford paused for only a moment before he followed her. But he did have one last thing to say to Mr. Plimpton.

"You will regret this."

The sound of Mr. Plimpton's mocking laughter followed them all the way to the street. "We shall find you another publisher," Stamford told Tessa reassuringly.

But it was not so easy as Stamford had thought. To be sure, there was some interest. But as soon as they discovered the state of affairs with Mr. Plimpton, everyone they asked backed away from the notion of publishing Tessa's stories.

Hours later, greatly discouraged, they returned home, only to find Lady Rivendale had been and gone. "Did she say what her purpose was?" Tessa asked her aunt.

Miss Winsham shook her head. "No, and I did not press her to say. More of this foolishness, I suppose, about the books. Tell me, instead, what Mr. Plimpton said when you confronted him."

Tessa sank into the nearest chair and briefly described to her aunt what had happened. Stamford chimed in, from time to time, with his view of the matter. In the end, it was Miss Winsham who rose to her feet and paced about the room. She tapped her chin as she did so and muttered in dire accents about a proper revenge. There was a grim look in her eyes, and she frowned as she paced. But when she finally turned to speak to Tessa, it was in a perfectly ordinary voice, speaking perfectly ordinary words.

"No one knows you wrote those stories. And thank heavens for that small favor!"

"Lord Rivendale knows. And Lady Rivendale," Tessa pointed out.

Miss Winsham waved away the objection. "Yes, but it doesn't matter. Neither of them will betray you. What matters is that no one else discovers the truth. You must play the part of a fashionable young lady—one who has not a thought in her head for telling stories."

"That," Tessa said dryly, "will be rather hard to do. No one is likely to believe that I adore the round of social visits."

"They don't have to believe it," Stamford said slowly. "They need only believe that your sister and I are pressing you to find a husband. And it is we who are insisting you go out and about."

"Yes, tyrant that you are, no doubt everyone will believe such a Banbury tale," Tessa retorted.

But despite her sharp words she had to admit there was a certain sense to what he said. Still, as she went upstairs, her thoughts were occupied far more with wondering what Lady Rivendale had wanted than in imagining the next social affair she would attend.

On the other side of town, William was furious. He had read the offending volume, the latest story from the notorious lady of quality—the one everyone had been talking about last night. And he had recognized both himself. For that he found it hard to forgive Miss Barlow.

And yet he also found it hard to believe she could have perpetrated such a mean-spirited trick upon him. He would have sworn they were friends. And she had certainly seemed distressed to hear the gossip last night, at his mother's party. Surely if she had written the book this way, wishing to cause a scandal, she would have reveled in such talk.

But it was Miss Barlow's book. And if she had not done so, then who had made these scurrilous changes to her story? The answer came to him instantly—Plimpton. Recollecting the publisher, Rivendale found it far easier to believe that somehow that fellow had been behind the change in Miss Barlow's stories than that she had betrayed him in such a way.

And so, although he was upset, William found himself defending the unknown author that evening, when a fellow member of White's began to disparage her.

"No doubt she's a bitter, dried-up spinster. P'rhaps aunt to more nieces and nephews than she can count. And dislikes every single one of them," the man said, prompting laughter from his companions.

"But if that were so, how does she know so many members of the *ton*?" Rivendale asked mildly. "I cannot think of any such spinster of my acquaintance."

"No?" someone else countered. "What of the spinster in the house you visit all the time?"

"Aye, Miss Winsham, isn't it? Who's to say she didn't write these books? You have been in her house a great deal. Who's to say she didn't take you in dislike and decide to mock you in her latest book?"

Rivendale felt a profound sense of dismay. He did not believe Miss Barlow had written her story the way it had been printed. But he could not say so without betraying her secret, without betraying that she was the author. But to have suspicion fall upon her aunt, Miss Winsham, seemed an equally bizarre nightmare, and he wondered how to extricate both of them from the net of suspicion that continued to tighten as the men murmured among themselves.

The conjecture might have been dismissed as utter nonsense save for one thing. A number of the men present had been subjected to the sharp edge of Miss Winsham's tongue, either when they called upon Miss Barlow or her sister or when they encountered the ladies at one social event or another. In short, these gentlemen wanted to believe that Miss Winsham was the one responsible.

Rivendale watched and listened a little longer, and then he turned away, afraid he might otherwise betray too much. Indeed, he was happy to make an early night of it. Tomorrow he was going to have to go and warn Miss Barlow and her aunt.

To be sure, if it turned out he was mistaken and she had written this nonsense, then he would find it hard to forgive her. But no matter what the truth, no matter how angry he might be with Miss Barlow, his sense of justice was too great to allow the blame to fall upon Miss Winsham's shoulders.

He was dismayed, the next day, to be shown into a drawing room that was full of callers. He could see from the avid expressions on their faces that they had come to see if Miss Winsham was indeed the authoress of these tales. It would seem that more than one person suspected her of writing them. And from the grim expression on the faces of Miss Winsham and her nieces, it was evident that enough had been said to make them realize where suspicion was directed. Miss Barlow's face was almost as pink as the rose-colored dress she wore.

With a deep breath, William stepped forward and greeted Miss Winsham with a friendly smile. "How do you do, today?" he asked. "Have you heard the latest rumors? It is the most diverting thing! Some think you had something to do with the children's books everyone is talking about. Of course, anyone who knows you as well as I do knows what nonsense it is to think such a thing."

He felt, rather than heard, the consternation behind him, and the relief from the Barlow sisters. As for Miss Winsham, she straightened in her chair and demanded, "Do you think I lack the wit to write such things, Lord Rivendale?"

He shook his head and, undaunted, took the seat beside her. "No," he said with a smile. "I know your wit to be remarkable. It is the lack of malice in your nature that makes such a thing unthinkable."

Was that a choke of laughter from one of Miss Winsham's nieces? Perhaps he had not chosen the best of examples, but those who did not know her so well might believe what he had said. Now there was a distinct murmur, as others hastened to assure Miss Winsham that they also did not believe the rumor that was so absurd.

By the time the last of the disappointed crowd left, within the half hour, William was beginning to feel tired from smiling so much. But he could not leave, not until he had a chance to speak to Miss Barlow alone. His chance came when the last of the other callers closed the door behind her, leaving him with Miss Winsham and her nieces.

"I thank you, Lord Rivendale, for your quick wit and your kindness in helping to put paid to these rumors," Lady Stamford said, coming forward to offer him her hand as well as a friendly smile.

"I could do no less," he said gravely. "Not when I knew Miss Winsham did not write those stories."

To his left William saw Miss Barlow flinch. It was her younger sister, however, who spoke up. "Neither did Tessa write those stories—at least, not the last one!" Lisbeth said hotly. "Not the way it was published. The publisher, Mr. Plimpton, made those changes. Without her permission. Sir Robert and my sister went to try to make him print the proper copies. And make a public apology."

William looked at Miss Barlow. He felt an absurd sense of relief at her sister's words. Aloud, however, all he asked was, "And *is* Mr. Plimpton going to make a public apology, and reprint your last book—the way it should have been printed?"

A look of both dismay and desperation crossed her face. She sank back into the chair behind her and shook her head. "No, he refuses. He insists he only made a few necessary *improvements*, as he calls them. He says I have no recourse in the matter. I have refused to give him any more of my stories, of course, but I have not been able to find anyone else willing to take them. I, too, thank you for coming to Aunt Margaret's aid. But, oh, how I wish it had never been necessary!"

Somehow William found himself kneeling beside Miss Barlow, taking her hands into his. He stared at the locket at her throat and then up into her face.

"You must not worry, Miss Barlow," he said. "This absurd rumor about your aunt will soon disappear. And the scandal over this latest book will be forgotten."

"But no one will publish my work," she said to him with a stricken face.

Gently he wiped a tear from her cheek. "Does it matter so very much?" he asked softly.

"Yes. Without my stories, what am I?" Tessa asked, her voice breaking. "Who am I? All I have ever wanted to do is write. And that is all anyone has ever thought me good for. If I do not write, what am I to do with my life?"

William never thought he would say the words until they were already out of his mouth, and by then it was too late to take them back. It was as if he heard himself speaking from a distance when he answered her by saying, "Become my wife. Be Lady Rivendale, my wife, and mother to my daughter Anna."

There was a stunned silence in the room for several moments, and William was only too aware that everyone was gaping at him. He could scarcely blame them. And then it got much worse. Miss Barlow pulled her hands angrily out of his. She leaped to her feet and glared down at him.

"How dare you roast me in such a way, Lord Rivendale? I thought we were friends! I would not deserve such a trick from you, even if I had written those stories the way Mr. Plimpton published them."

Now it was William who went very pale as he, too, rose

to his feet. He reached out a hand to Miss Barlow, and she backed away. He let it fall to his side and tried again.

"I am not roasting you," he said. "I am perfectly serious. I need a mother for Anna, and you like her as much, I think, as she likes you. You need a direction for your life. Why not become my wife? You have told me before that you do not wish to be forever dependent upon your sister's husband. Well, if writing is not to be your ticket to independence, Miss Barlow, then marry me. If you do, you will no longer be dependent upon Sir Robert."

"No—I shall be dependent upon you instead!" she flung at him.

"Would that be so terrible?" William asked quietly, afraid to hear her answer.

She stared at him for a long moment before she answered. It was with great reluctance that she conceded, "No, perhaps not. But why? Why me? You need a wife who is comfortable in social circumstances. Someone who can host dinner parties and musical evenings, and, oh, all sorts of events. Not someone who is afraid of her own shadow!"

Rivendale laughed. He could not help himself. This picture she painted seemed so absurd to him. "I don't care about dinner parties and musical evenings and all those other sorts of events! I want a wife and a mother for Anna, not a hostess, I assure you. That is the least of my concerns."

Still she looked unswayed. As he watched, she took a turn about the room. Then she looked at him and repeated the words she had said before. "Why? Why on earth would you wish to marry me?"

It was William's turn to hesitate, particularly as he suddenly became aware that they were not alone in the room. It was not, precisely, that he had forgotten, but rather that all his attention had been focused on Miss Barlow. Now he found himself unaccountably reluctant to speak openly before her sisters and her aunt. As though they recognized his reluctance, the three women moved toward the doorway.

"We shall be upstairs if you need us," Lady Stamford said hastily.

"Don't need us about, in your way, I'll be bound," Miss Winsham added gruffly.

"Upstairs. Yes, we're going upstairs. Right now," the youngest, Lisbeth, added, pulling open the drawing room door as though frantic to escape.

When they were alone and William again dared to look at Miss Barlow, he discovered a smile tugging at the corners of her mouth.

"I am sorry," she said. "You should not have had to say any of this in front of my sisters or my aunt. But you need not fear that they shall hold you to what they overheard. I shall make it clear to them why it is impossible."

The smile gave William the courage to step closer and again take hold of her hand. "Is it so impossible?" he asked, with a wry smile of his own.

"Isn't it?"

William chose his words with great care. "I am not insisting that you share my bed, Miss Barlow. I understand we have not known one another long enough for you to feel comfortable with such a notion. To be blunt, I do not intend to have any more children."

"Not even an heir?" Miss Barlow asked.

She looked shocked, but William stood firm. "Not even an heir," he confirmed. "Miss Barlow, I do not expect you to feel more than friendship and affection for me. I know only too well that I am not the sort of man to make a woman happy. But I need a wife to be mother to Anna. And I can think of no better choice for her. In turn, I would do my best to see that you were happy, Miss Barlow. And it would guarantee that all the rumors about your aunt would cease. How could anyone believe such a thing when they see what excellent terms I and my mother stand upon with her."

"Your mother!" Miss Barlow objected, seizing upon the excuse. "Will she not object? How can she wish to see you tied to me?"

"She will not object, not once I tell her about Mr. Plimpton," William promised grimly. "And she will be delighted that I have finally decided to marry again. She has been telling me for this six months past that I ought to be looking about me for a wife."

He watched as her hand stole up to clutch the locket at her throat. And he held his breath as he waited for her answer.

Chapter 10

Tessa stared at Lord Rivendale. Her hand clutched the locket at her throat, and she felt it grow warm under her touch. Could he really mean what he was suggesting?

Tessa had always told herself it was foolish to think she would ever marry. Foolish to think it was something to be desired, either. Not after the example her parents set, not when she remembered all too well the permanent unhappiness in her mother's eyes.

And yet, in a tiny corner of her heart, she had always wanted children. The greatest pleasure she had ever known had come when she helped her older sister Alex take care of some of the children that Aunt Margaret had rescued when they were still at Henley Hall. How could she give up that hope by agreeing to a marriage in which she would not share a bed with her husband? In fact, how could she agree to a union in which she would always know that her husband felt no more than friendship for her?

Something of her emotions, though he misunderstood them, must have shown on her face, for Rivendale squeezed her hand, and there was an anxious look upon his own face as he spoke.

"I swear you shall never have reason to fear me. You have told me a little about your father. Enough for me to guess that is part of what holds you back. But I am not a man who will either gamble or drink to excess—no matter what lies you may have heard. And I will give you the freedom to do as you wish while you are my wife."

Tessa smiled wistfully, wishing he could know how his words hurt. Oh, she was grateful he wanted to marry her, and that he wished to make her as happy as he could. But it hurt that he could so misjudge the state of her heart. And yet, had she ever given him reason to guess that she felt more than mere affection for him? That she might someday wish to share his bed? The image rose in her mind, and a warmth stole through her, stirring feelings she had not known possible.

But she could say none of this aloud. Not when he had made it so clear that he did not want such emotions from her. Not when he believed he wanted this bloodless marriage he was proposing. So instead of speaking her heart, Tessa forced herself to draw in a deep breath.

Lord Rivendale was waiting for her answer. She must decide which was preferable—spinsterhood or a companionable existence with a man she was beginning to think she loved. Common sense told Tessa that she ought to walk away, to refuse him. Such a union would only tear at her heart every day that she lived in the same house with him, every time she heard his voice or saw his face.

Tessa opened her mouth to refuse, but instead she heard herself say, "Very well, Lord Rivendale. I should like very much to become your wife."

The smile that lit up his face warmed her, even if it was almost immediately replaced by an impassive expression and a gruff voice. "Er, excellent. I suppose we should inform your sisters and your aunt and Sir Robert. Indeed, I suppose I ought to ask his permission, but I cannot think he will object. I shall obtain a Special License, and we may be married as soon as you wish."

Tessa forced an equally impassive expression to her own face as she said, "Yes, of course. You can find Sir Robert in his library. I shall show you the way, and then go tell my sisters and aunt."

And so began what must have been one of the oddest betrothals in London. Even as she climbed the stairs to the floor above, Tessa found herself vowing that no matter what Lord Rivendale said, within a year's time she would be sharing his bed and his heart, just as a true wife should.

There might, after all, be practical reasons for their marriage, but that did not mean, she decided, that she need give up all her dreams. If she was going to marry, then she was going to marry in earnest, whatever Lord Rivendale's plans might be. And he would thank her. Eventually. She hoped.

If the interview with Sir Robert was difficult, it was nothing to the one William faced with his mother. Sir Robert had demanded to know finances, and what Lord Rivendale would do to protect Miss Barlow. He wished to discuss settlements, and he wanted an assurance that William would do his best to make her happy. Those were the easy questions to answer, easy things to promise, even if he did withhold some of the truth.

But Lady Rivendale regarded her son with far more piercing eyes and, because she knew him so well, much deeper doubts. William wanted to reassure her, but he could not lie, and soon the entire story of his proposal poured out. When he was done, his mother sat back, eyes closed, with an expression on her face as if she were in pain.

"Mother?" he asked, uncertainty in his voice.

She opened her eyes. "Oh, William, such folly!" she said sadly. "I wished to see you married. I like Miss Barlow. I even freely admit I have said you must find a mother for Anna. But this? It makes a mockery of the wedded state!"

Rivendale turned his back on his mother and went to stand at the window. She waited, and in the end, he was honest with her about this as well.

"I am not a man made for marriage," he said over his

shoulder. "You saw how unhappy I made Juliet. I do not think I am even capable of loving again. Because, you see, I did love her."

"I know."

The words were spoken softly, with so much understanding, that William felt close to breaking. He forced himself to speak gruffly.

"Then you know why I cannot offer any woman, any more than I have offered Miss Barlow today."

Lady Rivendale's response was not in the least what he expected. "No, I do not know why!" she thundered, slapping her hand flat against the table beside her.

William was so startled he turned to face his mother. He was taken aback by the anger he saw there, and even more so by her next words.

"What I know," Lady Rivendale said, rising to her feet and advancing upon her son, "is that Juliet did not know how to be a good wife. She was forever rushing about, or else laid down upon her bed in tears. She is the one who did not know how to love. You, William, loved too much. And that, I suspect, is what you are afraid of now. You are afraid that if you let yourself love again, you will be hurt again. And perhaps you will! There are no guarantees in this life. But if you do not risk such a thing, then you will never know the happiness your father and I knew together, and that, William, would be a terrible shame."

But her speech had given him time to take himself in hand. He met his mother's gaze steadily as he replied, when she paused for air, "You are mistaken. I understand why you would think as you do, but you are mistaken. I am simply being realistic. Fortunately, Miss Barlow is a sensible young woman and understands what you are not willing to accept. She and I will deal extremely well together, I assure you. And now, if you will excuse me, I must go upstairs and tell Anna the news. She will be delighted, and that, Mother, must make any other consideration irrelevant."

To her credit, Lady Rivendale let him go. That he saw a gleam in her eyes that he distrusted was something William preferred not to think about. For now his concern must be Anna. She must hear the news from him, not from one of the servants. Rivendale grinned to himself as he pictured how happy the news would make her. And that, perhaps, was the real reason he wanted to tell her himself.

Up in the nursery, Nanny was helping Anna with her letters. William watched for a moment from the doorway, so proud of his little girl. She might not yet speak, but he still hoped that would come in time.

As though she sensed his eyes on her, Anna looked up and saw her father. She jumped up from her chair and ran to him. She lifted her arms, demanding that he pick her up. With a laugh, William did so. He could deny her nothing, no matter how disapprovingly Nanny glared at him.

"I have news, Nanny," he told the older woman.

"And I suppose it could not wait, sir?" she demanded tartly.

"I think not," William answered gravely.

He set Anna back on her feet and led her to her chair, then took Nanny's chair and pulled it around to face his daughter. He took her hand as he tried to decide how to begin. In the end the words just came tumbling out.

"Anna, you are going to have a new mother. Miss Barlow and I are going to be married. You are going to be able to see her every day, instead of just once a week."

Behind him, Nanny gasped and then said, "Heaven be praised! It's about time the child got a new mother. I wish you every happiness, sir."

"Thank you," William told her, but he kept his eyes on his daughter.

Anna didn't seem to be as happy as he had expected she would. In fact, as he watched, her expression grew more and more mutinous, and finally she jumped up from her chair again. But this time, instead of running to him, she backed away, shaking her head in denial of the news.

"Yes, Miss Barlow and I are getting married," he repeated, thinking that perhaps his daughter simply didn't understand. "Miss Barlow will come and live here with us. She really will be your new mother."

Now Anna's head shaking became even more pronounced. She began knocking chairs over and sweeping papers off the table. Still she kept shaking her head.

Nanny ran to the child. Anna tried to push her away, but Nanny would not allow her to do so. She picked the child up and said to Rivendale, "Perhaps it would be best if you left us alone, sir. She needs time to become accustomed to the news, that's all."

William rose to his feet. He did not try to hide his bewilderment as he said, "I thought she would be happy! Why is she so upset?"

"I don't know, sir, and the poor wee thing cannot tell us. But she likes Miss Barlow, that I do know, and once she's here and married to you, Anna will have to come around. Just you wait and see, sir. Everything will work out."

William nodded. "I hope so."

And he left the nursery. He did hope Nanny was right. But Anna's reaction worried him. It was for his daughter's sake that he had asked Miss Barlow to marry him. And if his daughter wasn't going to be happy with the arrangement, then what was he to do?

It was, of course, too late to retract the proposal. By now Sir Robert would have sent the notice to the papers. And in any event, Rivendale knew the rules far too well. Once a proposal was given and accepted, a gentleman could not, in good conscience, withdraw it. And, he realized with some surprise, even if he could, he did not wish to do so.

That, however, was a thought William preferred not to dwell upon. He was betrothed, and Anna would simply have to accept that it was so. As Nanny had said, surely the child would come around once Miss Barlow was here in the house. All it would take, surely, was for Miss Barlow to tell her a story or two and Anna would be as happy in her company as she ever was. That was what Nanny thought, and after all, she knew Anna better than anyone, didn't she?

Downstairs Rivendale found that his mother was not so sanguine in the matter as Nanny had been. Nor was she surprised at the child's response.

"Well, what did you expect, William?" Lady Rivendale asked with some exasperation. "Anna still misses Juliet! How can you think she would welcome the thought of someone taking her mother's place?"

"But she likes Miss Barlow," William protested.

"Yes, as a visitor. Not as someone expected to usurp Juliet's place in her heart."

"But I don't expect anything of the sort," he answered. "Only for Anna to accept Miss Barlow as my wife, and as the woman who will now be responsible for her."

Lady Rivendale stared at her son, and he had the grace to blush. Rather than press the point, however, she took a somewhat different direction.

"Perhaps it is precisely her fondness for Miss Barlow that troubles Anna," Lady Rivendale suggested thoughtfully.

"What?"

"Perhaps," Lady Rivendale said, clearly feeling her way, "Anna likes Miss Barlow so much that she feels guilty. Perhaps she feels she ought to be more loyal to Juliet. And so she cannot admit that she would like Miss Barlow to be her mother. I remember, you see, how little patience Juliet had for Anna, except as a pretty, living doll whom she could dress in gowns that matched her own, so that when she took her out people would stop and exclaim what a pretty pair they made together. If that is the case, it will be very hard for Anna to accept this change."

"Do you think I should tell Miss Barlow that I have made a mistake?" William asked reluctantly.

Lady Rivendale studied her son. Finally she shook her head. "You cannot live your life for Anna. Besides, I do think that of all the young women I know, Miss Barlow would make the best mother for Anna—even if it is difficult for the child to accept at first. No, you cannot draw back, and I do not think you should. This marriage is not quite what I would have wanted for you, but who knows if it will stay that way."

And then, before William could ask what the devil his mother meant by that, she sailed out of the room with a murmur about appointments.

All Rivendale could do was sink into the nearest chair and wonder if he, or perhaps the whole world, had spun out of control.

Chapter 11

If the *ton* was surprised at the news of the betrothal between Lord Rivendale and Miss Barlow, there was also approval. He was a man who was liked by both men and women, and the general consensus was that it was past time he chose a mother for his child.

To be sure, Miss Barlow was an awkward creature, and her father, Lord Henley, had not quite been up to snuff, but she would do. The *ton* was much more interested in discovering the author of that scandalous children's book, anyway.

The wedding was a small one, held at a little church in a quiet part of town. Lady Rivendale would have preferred a more ostentatious affair, but under the circumstances, she conceded that perhaps her son was wise to be discreet. And his uncle, who had come to town for the wedding, was just as glad not to have to deal with a crowd.

Still, Lady Rivendale could not entirely refrain from meddling. As Tessa waited in a quiet room at the church for the wedding to begin, and her sisters twitched at the skirt of her gown and fiddled with her hair, Lady Rivendale slipped into the room. Alex and Lisbeth decided they ought to leave the two women alone. Thus it was that Tessa found her nervousness over the wedding suddenly increased tenfold, as she waited to hear what Lady Rivendale wished to say.

The older woman took some moments to study Tessa, and then she suddenly smiled. "You don't mean to accept this farce of a marriage, do you?" she asked.

"W-w-what do you mean?" Tessa stammered. She looked down at her gown. "I have every intention of exchanging vows with Lord Rivendale today."

Lady Rivendale waved a hand dismissively. "That is not what I meant. Of course you are going to marry him today. Only a fool would draw back when everyone knows the ceremony is supposed to take place shortly. No, I meant that you do not mean to accept my son's determination to keep this a passionless match with separate bedrooms and no feelings. Or do you?"

Tessa countered with a question of her own. "Do you think I should?"

"Heavens, no!" Lady Rivendale exclaimed. "I think you should do everything you can to shake my son out of his complacency. I shall be delighted if you can wake those emotions he tries so hard not to feel. But I had to see for myself that your feelings were engaged. These past days, you always looked so prim and proper when I saw you that I could not tell if you were intending as bloodless a match as he was."

Tessa sank into the nearest chair. She stared at her hands and then at Lady Rivendale. "I love him. I know that isn't fashionable, and it isn't at all what he wants. And if the only terms upon which I can have him are his bloodless ones, as you put it, then that is what I will have to accept. But, yes, I do hope to shake his complacency. Heaven forgive me, but I am hoping that in time he will want me in his arms, in his bed. And that he will allow himself to begin to care. At least a very little."

Lady Rivendale laughed softly. "Oh, my dear! William cares more than a little! What do you think scares him so much? He adored Juliet, his first wife, and she nearly broke his heart. He is terrified that if he admits to himself he cares for you, you will do the same. But I do not think you will."

Under the older woman's steady gaze, Tessa rose to her feet and came to stand closer to Lady Rivendale. In a voice that was utterly calm she said, "No, I would never hurt your son. Not if I could help it. I do mean to be a good wife to him, Lady Rivendale."

The other woman placed a hand on Tessa's arm and smiled. "I know you do, my dear. It is the one thing that reconciles me to this match. You will lead him a merry dance, but a very different one than Juliet did. And I shall watch with pleasure as you do. Perhaps you will be the one to bring him truly back to life again."

"Will you tell me about it?" Tessa asked. "What happened to his first wife? And, even more, I should like to hear about Lord Rivendale's childhood. I should like, you see, to know all that I can about him."

"You call him Lord Rivendale? Not William?" his mother asked with some dismay.

Tessa swallowed hard. "I tried, once, after he asked me to marry him, to call him William. He said . . . he said that he thought it better if we remained on more formal terms. He insisted that I should call him Rivendale."

"But in your heart he is William to you?"

"Yes."

"Good. Then here is what you need to know. William's first wife, Juliet, died in a carriage accident. She had Anna with her and the child was thrown free, but Juliet was killed instantly. He loved her far more than she was able to love him. Her loss was horrible for him, and even worse was the fact that Anna has not spoken since."

"How sad. Did it happen here, in London?"

"No, at our estate. That is why William refuses to go back there. I hope that someday he will change his mind. He was so happy there as a child. He hated it when we sent him off to school and couldn't seem to wait for summers and holidays to come home. And now he cannot bear to visit the place at all."

"I cannot blame him," Tessa said thoughtfully. "If I had

lost someone I loved in such a way, I should be reluctant to go there too."

"Reluctant, but you would do it, I suspect," Lady Rivendale said with a tiny, sad smile. Then, more briskly, she added, "But you asked about William's childhood. We haven't much time, so I shall tell you the most important thing for you to know is that my husband, the late Lord Rivendale, was a wonderful but also a most impractical man. If William had not taken over the reins of the estate at a very young age, there might not have been much left for him to inherit when my husband died a few years ago. It taught him to be a trifle high-handed and to value his judgment. Which would not be a bad thing, except when it means he will not listen to the advice of anyone else."

There was a knock at the door, and Lady Rivendale rose to her feet. "We had best go. They are waiting for us, and we shouldn't want to give William time to change his mind and flee the church!"

Laughing together, the two women swept out of the room. Everyone was waiting for the ceremony to begin, and in less time than she would have thought possible, Tessa herself became Lady Rivendale.

Lady Rivendale. She repeated it to herself silently. The name rolled strangely off her tongue. And she found herself worried by Anna's absence at the church.

Had Lord Rivendale told Tessa the truth about his daughter's feelings, she would have worried even more. But he had fobbed her off with excuses of a mild fever and minor indisposition. Indeed, he had taken care not to let Tessa see his daughter since the day he had told his child the news.

Tessa, therefore, had no notion the extent of Anna's rebellion. And the last thing she expected was the welcome she received from the child when, after the wedding breakfast at Sir Robert's town house, they arrived at Rivendale's home.

The servants were lined up at the front door, ready to be

introduced to their new mistress. Some had seen her before, of course, either the first time she came to read to Anna or on the evening of Lady Rivendale's soirée. But there were many who had no notion what the new mistress might be like. There was, therefore, a distinct undercurrent of excitement among the servants, as Tessa went down the line, greeting each one in turn, as Lord Rivendale introduced them to her.

Eventually, however, all the servants had been greeted and Rivendale took her to the drawing room, where his uncle and his mother were already waiting. Only then was Tessa able to ask again about Anna.

With a sigh, Rivendale nodded. "I'll have Nanny bring her down."

And that was when the real trouble began. The moment Nanny led Anna into the drawing room, the child began to kick and bite at the hand that held her arm in such a firm grasp. As Tessa watched with disbelief, Anna pulled free and tried to run to the doorway. But Lady Rivendale had anticipated her granddaughter's reaction and blocked the way.

Anna whirled, looking for another way out. Tessa watched with utter bewilderment. "What is the matter with Anna?" she asked.

At the sound of Tessa's voice, Anna looked at her—but only for a moment. Then she looked away. She grabbed up the nearest object and threw it in Tessa's direction. Rivendale moved to stand protectively between his daughter and his wife. Nanny began to threaten what she would do to Anna once she had her safely back upstairs. Lord Rivendale's uncle merely watched from the corner of the room and shook his head in marked disapproval.

Tessa ignored all of them. She moved as swiftly as she could to Anna's side and caught the child up in a firm embrace. She lifted her up so that the child had no way to escape. She made soothing sounds as she did so, her mind awhirl with conjecture. What was going on? And why had no one, including Lady Rivendale, warned her?

"Hush, little one, hush," Tessa kept repeating over and over until Anna finally went limp in her arms, exhausted, no doubt by her fury.

When she was certain Anna wasn't going to struggle anymore, Tessa found a nearby chair and sat cradling the child on her lap. Still she made soothing sounds. In the end, Anna's hand crept up to tuck itself into Tessa's, and she gave a tiny sigh of relief.

Over Anna's head, Tessa looked from Rivendale to Lady Rivendale, both of whom had somewhat guilty expressions upon their faces. Nanny, her face pale with worry, came forward and reached for the child.

"Let me take her now, m'lady. She's all tired out and will nap. Mayhap tomorrow she will be better."

Tessa hesitated, then nodded. She handed Anna over, relieved to see that the child did not struggle. "Yes, let her nap," Tessa agreed.

"We, er, that is, I am certain you and William wish to be alone," Lady Rivendale said. "Come, Cecil, let us give the newlyweds their privacy."

Rivendale's uncle seemed happy to oblige Lady Rivendale and they, too, left the room, albeit with far more haste than Nanny and Anna.

When they were alone, Tessa faced Rivendale. "What is going on?" she asked, wondering if the exhaustion she felt was evident in her face and hoping that it was not.

He did not at once answer, but Tessa waited. Finally, he said slowly, "My mother thinks that Anna is afraid you will try to take *her* mother's place, and she is not ready to accept such a thing."

"Well, of course she may feel that way," Tessa said, with pardonable exasperation. "But why did you not warn me? I would have spoken with Anna before the wedding and tried to help her understand. It would undoubtedly have been easier for her if I had."

"I did not wish to scare you off," Rivendale replied.

He said it as if it was a jest. But the jest fell flat, as he must have known it would. At the look upon Tessa's face, he made another attempt to explain.

"I thought that Anna would, that she must, come to accept our marriage. My daughter is very fond of you, Theresa. I know she is. I thought that once you were here, she would accept what she cannot change."

Tessa laughed, and it was not a happy sound. "She is a child! She would not think in such terms. All Anna knows is that her beloved father did not listen when she tried to let him know how unhappy she was about his decision."

As she spoke, Rivendale's face grew more and more austere. "Anna is my daughter. She will accept you. I have told her that she has no choice."

"And that is supposed to help?" Tessa asked incredulously. "You cannot control a child's emotions. You cannot control anyone's emotions!"

Tessa paused and took a step toward Rivendale. She reached out and touched the side of his face. Her voice softened as she went on, "We each feel what we feel, William. Can you not understand that?"

He stared at her, unblinking, and in his eyes she could see a profound grief. For a moment Tessa thought perhaps she had reached him. And then he spoke, his voice more grim, more austere than ever.

"I have told you before, ours is not that sort of marriage. It is far better if we maintain a certain formality with one another."

Tessa stepped back. "I see. But you have called me Theresa."

He nodded. "I am your husband. It is appropriate that I should do so. But I should prefer if you call me Rivendale—particularly in public."

"I see," she repeated, not knowing what else to say. And then, before he could say another word to feed her anger, Tessa brushed past him and out of the room. He made no move to stop her.

In the hallway she found Lady Rivendale waiting for her. That was when Tessa realized she had no notion where she was going. She didn't want to ask for her help, but the only alternative would have been to seek out a servant, and that would have been far worse.

"Lady Rivendale," she said, trying to keep her voice calm, "will you show me to my room?"

"Of course, my dear."

Lady Rivendale was obviously too wise to say a word in defense of either herself or her son. Instead she kept up a steady stream of advice about the household, and the servants in it. And once she had shown Tessa to the cream-and-pale-blue bedchamber that had been prepared for the new bride, the older woman withdrew.

"For I know you will wish to rest," Lady Rivendale said, starting to pull the door closed behind her. "It has been a most unusual and exhausting day for you, I'll be bound. I shall look forward to seeing you at dinner, my dear. And then, tomorrow, William's uncle and I leave for our country home."

And then Tessa found herself alone. More alone, she thought with dismay, than when she was in Sir Robert's house. There, at least, she had always had Lisbeth or Alex to turn to, or Aunt Margaret. Even, upon occasion, Sir Robert himself. Here she had no one. Lady Rivendale and William's uncle were about to leave, and her husband was turning out to be someone she didn't even know—not if he could have hidden Anna's distress from her, not if he could ignore it, as it seemed he had.

Tessa looked around the room. It was a comfortable one, and someone had taken the trouble to be sure it was welcoming, for there were fresh flowers on the nightstand. And

the staff was clearly efficient, for her things had already
been unpacked and put away. There was nothing sensible
left for her to do but to follow Lady Rivendale's advice and
rest.

But Tessa didn't feel like being sensible. Instead, she
reached for the writing desk that had been delivered to her
room. Lady Rivendale's notion, no doubt, and for that kindness she was grateful. Now she drew out paper and ink and
a fresh pen. And she began to write a story very different
from any she had written before.

Had any of the Rivendales been able to see what it was
she was writing they might have been alarmed. To be sure,
when she was done, her anger written out, Tessa took the
pages, ripped them up, and tossed them into the rubbish
bin, but the Rivendales still would have been alarmed. As it
was, they felt only relief at the respite from the anger of
both the youngest and the newest members of the household.

Chapter 12

It was early the next morning when Tessa entered the nursery. Nanny looked up in surprise at the sight of her, but Tessa put a finger to her lips to warn the other woman not to speak. Anna sat with her back to the door, and she seemed happy enough.

Tessa risked coming into the room, one small step at a time, until she stood very close to the child. Then she knelt beside the little girl.

"Anna?" she said softly. At the child's look of alarm, Tessa hastened to add, "I know you're upset. And I don't blame you. I should have been upset myself if someone had tried to bring a new mother into the house after mine died."

Anna froze in place, her expression a mixture of the fury with which she had begun to react and the desire to cry that followed. Tessa reached out and drew the girl into her arms. She cradled Anna's head against her breast as she stroked her hair.

"It's all right, Anna. I won't expect you to call me Mama. Or to think of me as one. I am married to your father, and I will be living here. I hope we will again be able to be friends, but I do not ask that of you until you are ready. I just want you to let me comfort you when you need someone to do so. Is that possible?"

Anna pulled back and looked up at Tessa. There was such confusion in her eyes that it broke the young woman's heart. She wished she could take away Anna's pain, though she knew that only time could perform that miracle. But when Anna once again rested her head against Tessa's breast, she let out the breath she had not even realized she was still holding. And Tessa risked hugging the child.

Then, knowing that she had no choice, Tessa let her go. Anna hesitated. She slowly backed up, then sat in her chair and began once again to work on the lessons she had been doing before Tessa came into the room.

Nanny and Tessa exchanged speaking glances. The older woman surreptitiously wiped away a tear. She followed Tessa out to the hallway. There she spoke in low tones so that Anna could not overhear.

"The child needs you, and that's a fact," Nanny told Tessa. "For all she pushed you away yesterday, she needs you. It's the best thing Lord Rivendale has done, bringing you into this house. Give her time, my little Anna, and she'll come around. Indeed, I'd say she's already begun."

"Thank you. I hope you may be right," Tessa answered with some constraint. "But I do not expect miracles overnight. Anna is, I think, a very frightened and a very angry child. How could she not be? I shall be satisfied if she simply ceases to push me away."

Then, understanding one another perfectly, Tessa and Nanny parted company, and Tessa went downstairs to say good-bye to Lady Rivendale and William's uncle, Cecil Rivendale. Even from up here, near the top of the house, she could hear the chaos in the foyer. Tessa smiled as she realized that Lady Rivendale was giving her son instructions on matters he no doubt knew as well as she.

"Ah, there you are, my dear," Lady Rivendale said, coming forward to embrace Tessa when she finally reached the bottom of the stairs. "I was hoping I would see you to say good-bye. I would not desert you, with Anna so upset, but every newly married couple needs privacy."

"Even if they aren't quite certain what to do with it," Cecil Rivendale chimed in, hugging Tessa in turn.

"Mother. Uncle," William said, in a voice full of meaning.

They merely smiled at him. "Yes, yes, we know you are impatient to be alone with your bride," Cecil Rivendale said, waving a hand carelessly. "We shall be gone as soon as the luggage is loaded onto the carriage. And then you can be alone with your bride. Kiss her in private as much as you wish. Don't want us hanging about for that!"

"That isn't what I meant," William said through clenched teeth.

"It ought to be!" his uncle retorted unrepentantly.

In spite of herself, in spite of her worries about Anna, Tessa found herself laughing. Cecil grinned at her, pleased with the results of his sally.

Rivendale threw up his hands in a gesture of surrender. His mother patted his arm understandingly. "We shan't tease you anymore, dear," she said. "Well, at least not for this visit. I hope matters will work out well for both of you. But that is, after all, your affair, not ours. I hope you will write to me, Theresa, and tell me how you go on as mistress of this house and mother to Anna."

"You may be sure that I shall," Tessa assured Lady Rivendale.

And then it was time for them to leave. William moved to stand beside Tessa on the top step as he watched the heavy traveling coach pull away from the curb. He stood close enough for Tessa to hear his sigh.

"You'll miss them, won't you?" she said.

He nodded. "My uncle is a recluse, but a brilliant one. And my mother is, well, my mother. And when I look at her, I think of my father, for I cannot picture one without the other. They were so fond of each other, scandalously so, some said. And they included everyone they met in their happiness. That is what I once hoped for myself."

Tessa wanted to suggest that perhaps, with her, he might still find it. But there was something forbidding in Rivendale's face, something that made her hesitate to break the moment's camaraderie.

Instead she said, "I, to the contrary, have never known such a couple. My parents were the most unhappy creatures I have ever seen, and that was what I always feared my fate would be if I married."

"Do you still fear it?"

Tessa turned to face Lord Rivendale. "If I had thought so, I would not have agreed to marry you."

He nodded, satisfied. Then he took her arm to draw her inside the house, for, as he said, "There is a cold wind out here, and I should not want you to catch a chill."

Tessa went willingly, wishing that they might always have this peace between them.

But before she could voice the words aloud, Rivendale turned to her and said, "I am going out. I shall not be back for dinner. Have the cook prepare anything you choose."

Then he was gone, and it was all Tessa could do to keep from bursting into tears.

Out on the street, William hesitated. He had told Tessa he was going out, not because there was anywhere else he wished or needed to be but because he could not bear the feelings she had stirred in him as they watched his mother and his uncle leave. The hope he had begun to feel, the things he had begun to wish for, were far too painful to contemplate.

As it was, however, William had no destination, no place where anyone expected him. If he went to his usual haunts, he knew there would be all sorts of questions he could not and did not wish to try to answer. Questions such as why he had left his bride of one day alone.

Maybe that was why William ended up on Sir Robert's doorstep. That gentleman took one look at Rivendale's face and immediately poured him a glass of brandy.

"Bit early in the day, isn't it?" William asked doubtfully as he took the glass.

Stamford grinned. "Not when a new bridegroom has that look on his face! Dished already, are you? Well," he added before Rivendale had time to take offense, "so was I, quick enough. Devil of a thing, marrying, isn't it? Though you've had practice. I was an utter novice when I married Lady Stamford. Not the slightest notion what I was about."

Despite his reservations, Rivendale found the brandy warmed the cold spot in the pit of his stomach that had been there since the day before. And when Sir Robert continued to regard him with a kindly expression on his face, William somehow found the courage to say the things he hadn't quite dared say to anyone else.

"What if I can't make her happy, Stamford? What if Anna won't accept Lady Rivendale as her mother? What if they both come to hate me?"

"And you think I have the answers?" Sir Robert asked with some surprise.

"I don't know if anyone does," William answered honestly. "I suppose I'm just thinking aloud and hoping you will have some advice." Stamford hesitated and Rivendale pressed the point. "How do you keep Lady Stamford happy?" he asked.

Sir Robert grinned. "I doubt she'd want me to tell you everything. But one piece of advice I can give you. Never argue with your wife. No matter what she says, she must be right. It will come to that in the end, so there is no point in trying to put it off. Might as well just agree with her right from the start."

Rivendale blinked, taken aback. "But that's what I did with my first wife. And it didn't work."

"Then perhaps," Sir Robert said, leaning forward and resting his hands on his desk, "the fault was in your first wife, and not in you." He paused, then added carefully, "I have heard it said that your wife was the gayest of creatures, and I have heard she was a tormented soul. I have heard she was both before she even met you. Perhaps you take too much blame for either upon your shoulders."

William started to object, stared at his host, stared at his empty glass, and then said, "Perhaps I had better have another."

In another part of town, Miss Elizabeth Barlow and Miss Winsham were staring with dismay at the clerk in a dry goods shop.

"Surely it cannot be quite so dear!" Lisbeth objected. "Back home the ribbon would be half the price."

"Then I suggest," the clerk said, not troubling to hide his disdain, "you had best go back home to get it."

"Come, we shall try another shop," Miss Winsham said in august accents that fooled no one but managed, perhaps, to salvage a little of her pride.

Outside the shop, however, her shoulders drooped, just a trifle. "Perhaps," Miss Winsham said doubtfully to her niece, "we ought to ask Sir Robert to increase the allowance he has been making you."

"No!" Lisbeth exclaimed with great determination. "I am too far in his debt already. You cannot know how greatly I dislike being the object of his charity."

Since Miss Winsham shared these sentiments, she could not disagree. Instead she said briskly, "When one has no other choice, it is foolish to refine too greatly over one's circumstances."

"Unless one can, by doing so, find a way to alter those circumstances," Lisbeth muttered obstinately.

Since Miss Winsham knew very well that there was no practical way for her niece to alter her circumstances, she very properly ignored the outburst. She tried, instead, to give her niece another direction for her thoughts by suggesting that they walk through the nearest park.

"For we are neither of us accustomed to being cooped up

in a house all day," Miss Winsham observed dryly. "Come, it will do us good to walk."

Had she had any inkling of how deeply Lisbeth's distress went, Miss Winsham might not have been so sanguine. She would certainly have tried harder to divert her niece. But since she did not, she congratulated herself on finding such an easy solution to their mutual dismal spirits.

And indeed, one could not walk among the flowers, or watch the children at play, without smiling. Nor did it hurt that Lord Thomas Kepley crossed their path. He spotted them long before they spotted him. Which was just as well. There were few things he hated more than to have people stare at him as he hobbled toward them, leaning for support on his cane. To be sure, his leg was getting better. He told himself every day that soon he would be on his way back to the Peninsula. But meanwhile, he preferred to come upon his friends unnoticed.

"Miss Winsham, Miss Barlow. Good day to both of you."

"Lord Kepley!" Lisbeth said with a smile. "How are you today?"

"Better," he said with a wry smile. "Particularly now that I have found the both of you and need not walk by myself."

But Miss Winsham noticed the way Kepley winced as he followed them, and she had a strong notion he had pressed himself too hard and ought to rest. "Why don't you and my niece sit over here?" she suggested, pointing to a handy rock. "I wish to speak to someone I know, and that way I will be able to find you when I am done."

Both Kepley and Lisbeth looked somewhat taken aback, but they did not protest and Miss Winsham felt a strong degree of satisfaction as she noticed the relief on Kepley's face when he took the weight off his leg. What they would find to speak of she neither knew nor cared. Perhaps they would raise each other's spirits. Besides, she truly did wish to speak to the woman she saw a short distance away. And she preferred not to have anyone overhear.

Meanwhile, Lisbeth attempted to put Kepley at ease, for she knew how much he disliked the limits his injury put on him, and the way everyone seemed to look at him with pity in their eyes. The trouble was, she had no notion what to say to him.

Fortunately, Lord Thomas Kepley had been through any number of Seasons and knew only too well how to coax even the shyest maiden to talk. By the time Miss Winsham returned, he had a fair notion of Elizabeth Barlow's circumstances, and her hopes and dreams for the future.

"I cannot like being dependent on my sister's husband," she confided with a sigh. "Sir Robert is all that is kind, but I do not like it, just the same."

"You could marry," Kepley suggested.

Lisbeth shook her head. "Never! I saw how unhappy my mother and father were. Nor do I want to place myself in any man's power, in such a way."

"Well," Kepley said lightly, "I have no great admiration for the state of marriage either. But if you do not wish to depend upon Stamford's generosity, and you do not wish to marry, what would you like to do?"

"You will think me foolish, but I like to be with children. I think perhaps I might make a good governess," Lisbeth said. "Except that neither my sisters nor Sir Robert will hear of it. And I cannot think anything else I have a talent for that they would find acceptable either."

And what could one say to that? Kepley was silent, as though he hesitated to tell Miss Barlow what he truly thought. Lisbeth put a hand on his arm.

"I have shocked you," she said.

"No!" Kepley replied, placing a hand over hers. "I am just sorry to hear of your circumstances."

"Oh, no, you ought not to be!" Lisbeth protested. "I am certain my foolish problems must seem like nothing compared to your injury."

Then, as though she realized perhaps she ought not to

have spoken of it, that he might not wish her to do so, she clapped her mouth shut and turned a fiery red. Kepley smiled wistfully.

"Do you know," he said, "that you are the only woman willing to speak of my injury? All the others pretend they cannot see it or that it does not exist. And yet I know from how they behave that it distresses them."

"Does it . . . pain you a great deal?" Lisbeth asked.

Kepley shook his head. "Only if I do more than I should. Which I will allow happens more often than I like. No, what distresses me most is that I know I am needed. To be sure, Wellington has any number of eager and qualified officers. But still, he could use a hundred more. Particularly those of us who have been there some time and know the realities of what we face."

"Is there any chance you will be able to go back?" Lisbeth asked.

A grim look played upon Kepley's face. "I shall go back. The only question is when. But that is something neither my surgeon nor my family wish to hear!"

They smiled at each other then and felt a mutual sympathy. From that point on, it was easy for Lisbeth to talk with Kepley, and that was how Miss Winsham found them when she returned.

Despite the evident discomfort to his leg, Lord Thomas Kepley insisted upon accompanying Lisbeth and Miss Winsham to the edge of the park and handing them into Stamford's waiting carriage. With a smile he declined their invitation to accompany them, pleading another engagement. Lisbeth and Miss Winsham returned to Stamford's town house just in time to see Lord Rivendale emerge.

"Sir?" Miss Winsham addressed him. "Is Theresa here as well?"

"Er, no, I left her at home this morning. I'm going back there now," Rivendale replied, pronouncing each word with exaggerated care.

He bowed, then set off down the street, his gait not altogether steady. Lisbeth and Miss Winsham watched with mouths agape.

"Aunt Margaret, was Lord Rivendale drunk?" Lisbeth asked when he was out of sight.

"I fear so," Miss Winsham replied grimly. "And I do not like seeing him in such a state this soon after the wedding. Come, let us go and see if Sir Robert can tell us what problem exists."

But when they found him, it was immediately evident that he was not in much better condition than Lord Rivendale, and by silent agreement Lisbeth and Miss Winsham withdrew without saying a word.

As they made their way up the stairs to their bedchambers, Lisbeth muttered, "I am never going to marry."

"Nor I," Miss Winsham agreed. "It is the most foolish of circumstances. Mind you, Alex seems happy enough. But she is the exception. You and I are far too wise to place our fates in the hands of any man."

And in perfect accord, the two women agreed to stay forever spinsters, taking care of one another, if need be. If Miss Winsham spared a thought for the locket that was passed through the women of her family, or wondered about the face she had once seen there herself, she did not say so aloud, and none could ever have guessed.

Chapter 13

The candles burned low. It was late, very late, and Rivendale had not yet come up to bed. Tessa clutched her robe tight at the neck. Was she making a dreadful mistake? Would he be angry with her for what she meant to do?

It didn't matter. They had been married for a week now, and things were no better between them. Lord Rivendale was always polite to Tessa. He escorted her to social events and publicly laughed away the rumors about the stories being written by Aunt Margaret. But he made no move to touch Tessa. Nor did he search out her company. Indeed, she was certain that he actively avoided her. It was a situation she found intolerable. So tonight she was determined to do something about it.

Slowly she let go of the top of her robe and allowed it to fall open. The night rail she wore was of sheerest lawn. Then Tessa brushed her hair until it gleamed in the candlelight. Mama had always said that men liked to see women with their hair down about their shoulders. She looked in the mirror. There was nothing more she could do, for she would not resort to artifice. No, if William—just this once she refused to think of him as Rivendale—were to come to want her, it would have to be for her true self.

With a candle in one hand and the other holding her robe closed, Tessa went out of her room and down the stairs, hoping all the servants had retired for the night. She very much feared her courage would desert her should she run into any of them.

But she didn't. She crept closer and closer to the library. That was where she thought Rivendale would be found. Yes, when she got close enough, she could see a little light spilling out from beneath the door. And when she silently opened that door, she could see that he was sitting in his favorite chair with his back to the door.

He must have heard Tessa, for as she came forward into the room, he rose from his chair. "You are up very late," he said, staring at her with a frown.

"No later than you," she countered. "I could not sleep. It would seem you share that problem."

Rivendale glanced down at the book in his hand. "I always read late," he said.

She nodded. "Perhaps I will join you."

"No! That is, are you not tired?"

"If I could sleep, I would."

"Take a book upstairs with you," he said, a hint of desperation in his voice. "Then, if you should become sleepy, it will be a simple matter to set your book aside and blow out your candle."

Tessa smiled wistfully. "It is lonely upstairs in my room. I should rather have your company as I read."

"I, er, yes, of course."

Tessa chose a book at random from his shelves. It did not matter what she read. She did not mean, after all, to be reading very long. Rivendale would have sat back down in his favorite chair again, but she forestalled him.

"Please sit beside me on the sofa," Tessa said. "I will feel better if you are close to hand."

He wanted to refuse, she could see it in his face, but in the end he came and sat beside her, just as she asked. He fumbled with his book, but seemed to find his page. Tessa pretended to be oblivious to all of it, as she opened her own book and began to read.

When she thought enough time had passed, she eased her knee over so that it brushed against his. Startled, Rivendale jumped a little. She pretended to keep reading. After a moment she felt him relax and, to her delight, he left his knee touching hers.

She waited. Then, when his breathing had calmed even more, she moved her arm so that it touched his. This time she could feel him turn to stare at her, but again she pretended to be engrossed in her book, and he did not pull away.

Finally Tessa closed her book and yawned. She closed her eyes as though very, very sleepy and set her head on his shoulder. Lord Rivendale went still. He held his breath, she thought, and if it would not have ruined her pretense, she would have held hers.

Just as she thought her plan had failed, she felt his lips brush against the top of her head, and she smiled. It was a beginning.

"Theresa?" he said softly.

She pretended not to hear.

"Theresa?" he said, giving her a tiny shake.

Still she pretended not to hear.

Rivendale slipped out from under her head, and still she pretended to be sleeping. Was he going to desert her? Go upstairs to bed and leave her here?

No, he lifted Tessa in his arms, cradling her gently against his chest. Then he blew out all of the candles and began to walk toward the doorway.

He must have known his house very well, for the darkness did not seem to daunt him in the least. He did not hesitate, as he walked the hallway and then began to climb the stairs to the bedrooms. He had to fumble a bit to manage to open her door, but he did, and then he carried her inside and laid her on her bed.

Tessa wanted very badly to reach up and pull him to her. But then he would have known she had not really been asleep, and she doubted he would forgive her for tricking him in such a way. No, she told herself, she must be patient. Little by little, she must coax him to her, as if he were a wild creature in need of taming.

Not that she wished to tame Rivendale. She only wanted him to come to realize what he was missing by holding her at arm's length this way. She wanted him to realize what he would gain if he let himself risk loving again, let himself risk caring again. And that would take time.

So when he set her on the bed and pulled the covers over her, Tessa only pretended to shift in her sleep. She did not reach out to him, nor did she speak. She only listened as he stood there in the dark, watching her.

To be sure, when he reached down and stroked her hair, Tessa permitted herself to smile. His hand stilled for a moment, and then withdrew. But she could hear the words he whispered in the dark.

"You are beautiful. I wish I could love you as you deserve."

Then he turned and left the room. She could hear his footsteps as he went down the hallway to his own room, could hear his door close, though he tried to be quiet.

It was all Tessa could do to keep herself from following him—from trying to go at once to join him in his bed. But she would give him time, she told herself. Time to think of how she felt in his arms, time to wish she was still there. Then, perhaps, when she came to him, he would welcome her. Half an hour, she thought, might suffice.

In his room, William stared up at the ceiling in the dark. He wanted so much to go back to Theresa's room. He wanted to join her in that large bed of hers and do all the things a man did with his wife. But he could not. He would not risk getting that close to anyone again. And he would certainly not risk having another child—one who might get hurt the way Anna had been hurt when Juliet died.

So he stayed in his lonely bed and counted all the reasons he was wise to do so. And when sleep still did not come, he counted the things he ought to be doing to take care of Anna. Among other things, he ought to find her a governess, for his mother had not done so, after all. He ought to have, before now, asked Tessa to do so.

Tessa. In the privacy of his own thoughts, William allowed himself to use the endearment that he would not let himself speak aloud. No, aloud he must always use the formal version of her name. Otherwise he would forget himself.

He shifted positions in the bed. He tried to remind himself of other commitments, other obligations he had to various friends that would keep him safely away from Tessa over the next few days. In short, he did everything he could to distract himself from thinking of her.

But of course it didn't work. He kept thinking how she had fallen asleep so trustingly on his shoulder. He could not imagine Juliet ever doing so. No, nor letting him carry her to bed. Bed—his bed, at any rate—was the last place Juliet had ever wished to be!

The odd thing was, William could picture Tessa in his bed. He could picture her there, smiling up at him, her hair spread about her on the pillow. Lord, her hair! It had been like a waterfall, cascading down her shoulders when she came downstairs. What the devil had she been thinking?

And what the devil was *he* thinking to picture her in his bed, smiling? It was nonsense, all nonsense. Ladies didn't smile in bed. Well, perhaps some ladies, but certainly not wives! All his friends told him so and Juliet never did. He had promised Tessa he would not ask her to share his bed. So he had no right to even think of such a thing in the first place.

But surely it couldn't hurt just to wonder a little if she would welcome him. Or whether she would pull back in disgust, as Juliet had done.

Perhaps it was because he was conjuring her up so clearly in his mind that William was not surprised when his bedroom door opened and closed and she, Tessa, slipped into bed beside him.

"I thought you were asleep," he said, certain that it was he who was dreaming.

"I did not want to be alone."

Surely it was his imagination that conjured up such words? Surely, therefore, it could not hurt if he stroked the soft brown hair at her temples and ran his finger down the side of her cheek?

He ought to send her away. But he could not be so cruel. He was dreaming, William told himself. That must be so. And in dreams anything was permissible. Even leaning over and covering her mouth with his, nibbling at the edges, savoring the taste, slipping his tongue inside to explore the silky depths.

Surely, in a dream, it was permissible, when she matched his fervor with her own kiss, to cup one breast gently with his hand. Surely it was permissible to thread his fingers through her hair and spread it out even more.

And if it were not, would she be reaching out to stroke his shoulder? Would she be threading her fingers through his hair? Real or dream, if she were offended, would she lift her night rail so that he could touch the soft roundness of her bottom?

If it was a dream he prayed he would not wake. If it was real he thought he was in heaven. And when the moment came that proved it was no dream, and that Tessa had never before known a man, he held her as if she were the most precious thing he had ever known. And she was.

Chapter 14

Tessa stretched, smiling to herself. To be sure, she was a little stiff, a little sore, but her heart felt more whole than it had in some time. The bed beside her was empty, but it had been her choice to return to her own room.

She had decided that she did not want William waking in the morning and thinking he ought to apologize. She did not want him to be entirely sure that what had happened was real. Let him wonder. Let him think of what had been—and wish for it some more. She would not make this easy for him. But then, he had not made it easy for her, either.

She wanted him to look at her and feel as if she was just out of reach. She wanted him to come to long for her touch, as she already longed for his. And to that end, she dressed in one of her more sober-hued gowns, of a dark green, and had her maid pin her hair up in the most forbidding style she could imagine.

As she looked at her image in the mirror, Tessa had to laugh. It did not seem to resemble very much the woman she felt herself to be. But that was all to the good. Let Lord Rivendale, let *William*, watch and wonder until he could no longer resist the urge to discover whether this woman or the wanton woman who had shared his bed in the middle of the night, was the real Tessa.

She found Rivendale in the breakfast room and greeted him as warmly as she always did. He mumbled a reply and looked down at his plate, as though the food there had great fascination for him.

Tessa smiled to herself. So that was how he wished to treat the matter? Very well, she could pretend to a similar indifference. She filled a plate for herself from the sideboard and then sat opposite her husband.

"Did you sleep well?" she asked in a placid voice as though she were asking about the weather.

He started and shot her a warning glare. "Did you?" he retorted.

She smiled. "I had surprisingly pleasant dreams. And did you?"

"I as well," he said in a voice that seemed to belie the words.

"I am pleased to hear it," Tessa said, in the same placid voice as before. "Have we any plans for tonight?"

"Plans for tonight?"

Rivendale positively sounded as if he were choking! Tessa hastily suppressed the grin that threatened to betray her knowledge of what she was doing.

"Yes, plans for tonight," Tessa said innocently. "I thought perhaps we could go to the theater. Unless, of course, we are expected somewhere else."

"I, er, no, no we are not expected anywhere else. The theater would be fine," Rivendale replied, rubbing his forehead with his fingertips. But he was beginning to recover. "Shall I invite your sisters and aunt to join us?" he asked.

"Why, that is a wonderful notion," Tessa agreed and favored him with a dazzling smile.

He stared at her as if she had grown two heads, and she carefully pretended not to notice. "Yes, well, I shall go and send around a note to ask them," Rivendale said, hastily rising to his feet.

"Thank you."

Tessa would have given way to the bubble of laughter in her throat if she had not been so aware of the interested eyes and ears of the servants. So, instead, she forced herself to consider her strategy. Trying to bring Lord Rivendale around, she decided, was not so very different from trying to coax Anna into accepting her.

The thought of Rivendale's daughter caused Tessa to finish her breakfast quickly. She had almost completed the story she had been working on, and if anything could coax the child out of her sullens, surely it would be finally hearing the ending. Tessa hoped so, for aside from the hug she had allowed that first day after her father brought Tessa home as his wife, Anna had not allowed her new mother near her.

At the sight of Tessa in the nursery door, Anna did as she always did. She carefully turned her chair so that she need not see her. Undiscouraged, Tessa sat down in a nearby chair and began to read where she had left off the last time she read this story to Anna. When she glanced up, from time to time, she saw Nanny watching and smiling. Anna obstinately kept her head bent over her desk.

Tessa kept reading. When she was done she swallowed the sigh of frustration she felt and began to roll up her manuscript. But before she could tie the ribbon around it again, a small hand reached for hers. In surprise, Tessa looked up to see Anna standing before her. When the child did not object, Tessa lifted her onto her lap. Anna patted the manuscript and Tessa began to read it all over again—this time from the very beginning.

That was where William found her. He stood for a long time in the doorway, watching. He did not fool himself into thinking all of the trouble with his daughter had been resolved, but nonetheless he sent up a fervent prayer of thanks that Anna was beginning to accept Theresa.

When he tried to think what their lives would be if he had not found Theresa, all he felt was a profound sense of loneliness. As he remembered the night before, he found

himself wanting to tell Theresa that he loved her. But he
could not. Not when he had failed so badly with Juliet.

Worse, William could mark the change in his first wife
from the day he had told her he did not think he could live
without her. From that day she had begun to do what she
wished, recklessly flouting both his wishes and the conven-
tions of the *ton*. How could he risk such a thing happening
with Theresa? It didn't matter how foolish his mind knew
such a fear to be, the fear was still very real.

And then she looked up. Theresa smiled at him, and
William could not help but smile in return. In that moment
there was, it seemed, a perfect communication, a perfect
sharing of happiness that Anna was sitting on Theresa's lap.

At that moment, Anna looked up, too. At the sight of her
father, and at the look he and Theresa exchanged, she
seemed to go wild, suddenly pummeling at Theresa and
throwing the pages of her story all over the floor.

Immediately William dashed to his daughter, reaching
her just before Nanny. She struggled in his arms even as he
tried to calm her down. Over her head, William could see
the stricken look on his wife's face. And the anguish as she
bent down to gather up the pages of her precious manuscript.

Nanny was scolding. "Anna! Stop that this instant! You
are not to behave like that! Anna!"

But the child would not calm down, no matter what any
of them said to her. That made it all the more frustrating
when a footman came in search of Lord and Lady Rivendale to inform them that they had callers below. He had to
hand his still struggling daughter over to Nanny and hope
the woman would be able to soothe her.

He guessed, a little bitterly, that Anna would calm down
the moment he and Theresa left the nursery. He wished he
knew what he could do to make his daughter accept the
choice he had made for the both of them. And after last
night, he felt the need to do so more urgently than ever.

In the drawing room, Theresa and William found Miss Winsham and Stamford pacing about the room. Both looked up and started to speak at once.

"There's been another book," Miss Winsham said without preface.

"I've already contacted my barrister for advice," Stamford added grimly.

"You've got to publish another story somewhere else to put the lie to this," Miss Winsham advised.

"I've just come from Mr. Plimpton. I told him to desist, but he only laughed," Stamford told them angrily.

William took one look at his wife's stricken face and guided her into a chair. Then he turned to Stamford and said, "I collect that Mr. Plimpton has brought out another volume, not one written by Theresa at all, and claimed it is by the same author as before."

"Precisely."

"And we cannot deny it or protest without revealing Theresa's identity," William went on, as much to himself as to anyone else.

"If I were a man, I would plant Mr. Plimpton a facer!" Miss Winsham said indignantly. "I wonder you did not do so, Sir Robert."

The two men exchanged speaking glances, and it was William who answered, in the most patient of tones. "I am certain Mr. Plimpton would have liked nothing better. He would have sent a description of the encounter to the papers, and then we really would be in the suds. No, we must look to other action to stop the man."

"I still think," Miss Winsham persisted, with a distinct sniff, "it would be best if my niece published another story on her own. Anyone seeing it would realize that this latest volume brought out by Mr. Plimpton is a paltry imitation."

"Yes, but we already tried. There are no other publishers willing to risk crossing Mr. Plimpton," Stamford pointed out gently. "Apparently he is as unscrupulous in dealing with competitors as he is in dealing with his authors."

"Well, surely you do not mean for us to tamely give up?" Miss Winsham demanded indignantly.

"No, not quite that," Stamford agreed. "I simply haven't hit upon a solution yet."

"Perhaps I have," William said slowly. "Let me make some discreet inquiries. In any event, it is for me to take action on behalf of my wife, not you."

"While you and Stamford discuss this, Lord Rivendale," Miss Winsham said austerely, "I should like to speak with my niece in private."

"Certainly."

Tessa led the older woman to a smaller parlor. Her aunt closed the door and moved as far away from it as possible. Only then did she explain.

"I don't wish you to worry, and I know that Stamford and William would worry, simply because they are men," Miss Winsham said. "But if something should happen to me, I want you to know that I wish you to go to the house you followed me to, a while back, and tell the people there."

There was no need to ask which house she meant—they both knew only too well. "Aunt Margaret, what is going on?" Tessa demanded.

"Nothing, nothing, my dear," the older woman said, waving her hands in a gesture of dismissal. "I just thought I would tell you that."

"I see," Tessa said dryly. "You know, of course, that I am not going to swallow such a plumper. Out with it, Aunt Margaret! What, precisely, are you involved with now? What were you hiding from me the day we were there? Something to do with children, I'll be bound. Does Stamford know you are adding to the list of young ones for whose welfare he will be responsible? And that you are putting yourself in danger?"

Miss Winsham looked away. "A few more young ones will be nothing to Sir Robert. His pockets, I daresay, are bottomless. And I did not say I was putting myself in danger."

"No? You simply tell me that if something should happen to you I should go to these people. Well, I am asking why you should fear that something will happen to you," Tessa said, making her voice as severe as she could. "What has changed since the day you and I were at that house?"

"I don't preciously fear that something will happen to me," Miss Winsham said cautiously. She paused and squared her shoulders. "I am, however, a practical woman, and it would be foolish to think it impossible that some of the people from whom we are rescuing these children will object. Perhaps violently so."

"Aunt Margaret!" Tessa exclaimed, aghast. Now she was on her feet, her voice urgent as she said, "You must not take such chances! Leave it to others to do so. Your part is surely sufficient in finding them a place to go!"

"Leave it to others?" Miss Winsham echoed, her voice scornful. "What others? Do you know how rare it is to find anyone who cares? Anyone who thinks it unconscionable, as I do, to place little girls in whorehouses? Or to force little boys to climb chimneys? Or worse, to mutilate some to make them beggars on the street? We could use a thousand more like me and it would still not be enough."

"But the risk!"

"Do you think I count it?" Miss Winsham demanded. "I understand your concern, Tessa, but I am going to do this. I told you not to seek your approval but only to give you a means to find out what happened if I disappear or fall prey to an accident of some sort."

Tessa began to pace about the room in some agitation. She knew her aunt too well to bother to argue. Once Margaret's mind was made up, she would follow it and damn the consequences—consequences that in this case could be fatal. Tessa did not like it, but she could not stop her aunt, either. Instead she tried to persuade her to caution.

"Can you not purchase the freedom of these children, rather than stealing them away?" she asked.

Miss Winsham regarded her niece with a great deal of exasperation and began to tap her foot. "What did you think I was doing?" she demanded impatiently. "Of course I try to purchase the children, rather than stealing them! Did you think I was an utter fool?"

"Then why," Tessa asked with a frown, "would you be in any danger?"

"Because these people, some of them, are perfectly content to take the money and then attempt to take back the boy or girl," Miss Winsham explained, as though to a child. "They have not the slightest scruples. And since they think I have none, that my plans for the children are at least as appalling as theirs, they think I would not go to a magistrate to stake my claim. And, in truth, since there is never a written contract between these people and myself I would have a hard time pressing my case. So usually I take someone with me. He's tall and strong and broad of shoulder. And so far it has answered. But as I said, I am a practical woman and I simply wish to take a natural precaution. Now may we drop the matter?"

When Tessa hesitated, Miss Winsham cursed fluently. Indeed, so fluent was she that had anyone in the *ton* heard even a tenth of what she said she would have been given the cut direct. But Tessa only laughed. This was Aunt Margaret, after all. A woman she had known all her life, and known all her life to be unconventional and eccentric.

When Tessa laughed, Miss Winsham smiled. "There, that's better. Good. Now, sit and tell me about Anna. She must be very happy to have you here."

Abruptly Tessa ceased to smile. "Not precisely," she replied. "She may have liked me as the lady who told her

stories, but she will not accept me as Rivendale's wife—
and her new mother."

"I see."

"What am I to do, Aunt Margaret? I dearly love the child
and I want her to be happy! I have tried everything I can
think of to set her at ease, but nothing works."

"Have you told her stories?"

"Of course I have!" It was Tessa's turn for exasperation.
"Just this morning I read her a story I had written. She sat
on my lap and seemed content until Lord Rivendale came
into the nursery. The moment she saw him, she turned into
a termagant and flung the pages of my manuscript all about
the room. Had there been a fire in the fireplace, my story
would have existed no more."

"Hmmm. Perhaps a soothing posset?" Miss Winsham
suggested. "I have managed to replenish my supplies somewhat, in the past few days, and I could send you something
you could brew into a drink for her."

Tessa shook her head. She knew her aunt's possets all
too well. At least by reputation. "No. I should like the child
to come to accept me of her own free will."

Miss Winsham started to object and then shrugged her
shoulders. "Very well," she said. "We shall have to think of
something else."

She was silent for several moments, and then she said,
"Have you shown her the locket?"

"The locket?" Tessa echoed, taken aback.

"Yes, the locket. You do still have it, do you not?"

"Well, yes, of course."

"Then show it to her. Children are fascinated by such
things."

Before Tessa could ask her aunt any more questions or
express her reservations, the door to the parlor opened and
Stamford poked his head into the room. "I, er, must be
going back to the house, Miss Winsham. Do you go with
me, or shall I send the carriage back for you later?"

"I'll come now," Miss Winsham said, rising briskly to her feet. To Tessa she added, "Remember what I said."

Then, before Tessa could ask whether she meant what she'd said about the locket or about her friends, Aunt Margaret and Stamford were gone. And Tessa, totally bewildered, went in search of William.

Somehow it seemed quite in keeping with the way the day had gone that he had already escaped the house. And her. Well, she thought with a sigh, she would see him and her sisters and Aunt Margaret again tonight, when they all went to the theater. Not that one could talk about serious matters there. But at least she would not feel quite so alone.

For a moment Tessa considered going upstairs and showing Anna her locket, but then she changed her mind. It was a ridiculous suggestion. After all, how could a locket change a child's feelings? And Tessa was reluctant, given Anna's behavior earlier, to risk letting the child near something that mattered so much to her.

Chapter 15

Tessa was quite right that the theater was not a place where one could discuss serious matters. But it was a place to be distracted, and she was grateful for that small favor. She watched her sister Alex and Sir Robert together, and noted the way they smiled at one another. She envied the way they seemed to find excuses to touch each other on the arm. The way they seemed to share so many thoughts that went unspoken.

Would she and William, Tessa wondered with a sigh, ever share such perfect companionship? Such was certainly not the case tonight! Indeed, Rivendale paid more attention to her younger sister, Lisbeth, than he did to her. Lord Thomas Kepley, whom William had invited to join them, paid more attention to Tessa than her own husband did. It was, she thought, a most lowering circumstance.

Nor could she talk to Aunt Margaret about what she had said earlier in the day, for the older woman took care to sit as far from Tessa as possible, on the other side of Lisbeth. With another sigh, Tessa resigned herself to being unable to accomplish anything, except to enjoy the performance. And it was an excellent performance. Despite her frustration, she could not regret asking Rivendale to bring her here tonight.

To be sure, it was a little unnerving to realize the degree of attention their box drew from other boxes, and even from the floor below. The *ton*, of course, was watching to see how Lord Rivendale treated his new wife, and she him. He was just attentive enough to satisfy their curiosity and spike any malicious rumors of incompatibility.

As for the patrons below and around them, Tessa could only think it was Lisbeth's pretty face, as she sat beside Aunt Margaret at the front of the box, that drew their attention. Several men seemed taken with her, and one man in particular kept turning to look up at their box. He looked to be a rather uncouth character, and finally Tessa whispered to her sister and Aunt Margaret to move their chairs a little farther back, which seemed to resolve the matter.

Still, at intermission, there was a steady stream of visitors to their box. Then, for the benefit of these visitors, Rivendale sat with his arm resting lightly on the back of Tessa's chair, and from time to time, he stroked her bare shoulder or her back above the neckline of her dress.

She shivered and wished he would never stop. Even more, she wished he was doing it not for show but because he wished to be doing it. That would truly have been bliss. But, like Aunt Margaret, Tessa was a practical woman, and she would take what she could get. If Rivendale would do this for show, then she would simply have to find as many opportunities as possible when he would want to show apparent affection toward her. And then perhaps in time the feelings would become real.

Meanwhile, she smiled and talked with those who came to the box. She found excuses to touch Rivendale on the arm, just as her sister Alex had touched Stamford. Abruptly she realized she really should have been paying more attention to the conversation around her.

"Daresay you've heard. Another volume out. More scurrilous than even the last one was."

In a bored voice Rivendale replied, "Yes, I know. Word has it that it isn't real."

"What the devil do you mean, it *isn't real*?" another man asked.

"Have you read it?" Stamford chimed in. "I think it a forgery. A poor imitation of the stories the lady was writing before."

"Indeed, I did wonder," a lady said thoughtfully. "But why would the publisher say it was by the same author if it was not?"

"Perhaps," Tessa said, as though the notion had just occurred to her, "there is something havey-cavey about the publisher? Perhaps she refused to write more stories for him, and rather than give up his tidy profits, he decided to publish someone else's work as hers?"

That prompted quite a few murmurs. Some held that no publisher would be so foolish. Others wondered aloud if it could be true. Neither group quite held a majority, but Tessa decided to give them more food for thought anyway.

"If this publisher were so unscrupulous as to bring out, under her name, a book the lady did not write," she said, "perhaps he altered the last volume as well. After all, in the first two books the lady wrote, there were no scurrilous elements at all."

How the debate might have gone, Tessa never knew, for the curtain was about to rise and their visitors had to hurry back to their own boxes. The moment they were alone, Rivendale squeezed her hand reassuringly and whispered softly into her ear, "Well done!"

"Well done, indeed," Miss Winsham said tartly.

She had, during the intermission, moved her chair to sit next to Tessa and now she was careful to keep her own voice pitched so low that even the others in the box could not overhear her. "Yes, you may stare, but I am not yet in my dotage, nor has my hearing yet begun to fail. It was well done so long as it does not prompt anyone to begin to suspect that you wrote those stories."

"Shhh," Alex warned.

"I see little danger so long as she says nothing more than she already has," Stamford added mildly.

And Tessa, who had had quite enough of the entire conversation, resolutely turned her attention to the stage. So
did the rest of the party.

Later, as they were making their way through the
crowded lobby to the street where their carriages would be
waiting, Tessa was jostled so much that her head began to
ache. She found herself leaning closer and closer to Rivendale, trusting him to keep her safe.

Perhaps she was a little off balance from doing so, but
suddenly she found herself pitching forward and could do
nothing more than put out her hands to break her fall.
Someone pushed past, shoving Lisbeth and Alex out of his
way as well. He would have collided with Miss Winsham,
but she was too nimble and managed to step to the side just
in time.

Stamford and Kepley both grabbed for the fellow and
missed, even as Rivendale tried to catch Tessa and keep her
from falling. Instead he merely succeeded in tearing the ribbon that trimmed her gown.

Voices started shouting. All Tessa could think of was that
she wished she were already home. Hands helped her to her
feet, and she saw with concern that Aunt Margaret looked
pale and both Stamford and Kepley looked very grim.

"You've torn your dress!" Lisbeth exclaimed.

"No, only the ribbon, I think," Alex countered. "And that
she may easily remedy with a new one."

"No manners, these young men!" Miss Winsham muttered angrily. "No manners at all. He didn't even stop to see
if you were all right!"

"Come, let's get you ladies home," Stamford said, starting to make a way for them again through the crowd.

"He's right," Rivendale agreed. "Lady Rivendale is still
very pale. I should like to get her into the carriage so that
she can sit down."

No one had any desire to object to such a sensible plan
and soon they were in sight of the carriages. Tessa and

Rivendale went one way, and Stamford and Kepley shepherded the others to Sir Robert's carriage a little farther back.

William was as solicitous as Tessa could have wished. He helped her settle against the well-cushioned squabs. He asked if she felt faint. He worried that her head might be hurting. He vowed to thrash the man if he ever saw him again.

And when they reached his town house, Rivendale accompanied Tessa up the stairs and to her bedroom door, his hand supporting her elbow the entire way. There he told her maid to make certain she went straight to bed.

That might have discouraged Tessa, if he had not reappeared soon after she was tucked under the covers. To be sure, he was hesitant and seemed to have to gather his courage to actually come and stand by the bed, but he did so.

"Are you all right?" he asked.

Tessa tried to smile and winced. Instantly he was sitting beside her and clasping her hand.

"If Stamford had succeeded in stopping the brute who knocked you out of his way, I'd have given the fellow a thrashing!" William said fiercely. "What would help? Shall I send for a physician?"

"No! That is to say, what I wish for, more than anything else, is your company."

Rivendale started to stiffen and withdraw, but Tessa would not let go of his hand. "You do not know what you are saying," he told her.

"I know precisely what I am saying, William," she countered. "What I cannot understand is why you should be so desirous of keeping a distance between us. After last night, I thought perhaps you would change your mind."

Now he really did pull free and move to stand by the window. Over his shoulder he told her sharply, "You do not know what you are asking of me. And I have told you before, you are to call me Rivendale."

"Even here, in my bedroom?" she asked, her voice soft and coaxing.

His voice shook, but he answered resolutely, "Especially here, in your bedroom! You think to make me change my mind, but I assure you, I am no fit husband for any woman. Not in the way that you want. We will only hurt one another, if we repeat what happened last night."

He sounded so sober, so despairing, that Tessa could not resist roasting him just a little. In a voice that seemed perfectly innocent she said, "Oh, but I thought—that is, Aunt Margaret told me—it would only hurt the first time. Was she mistaken?"

He turned now and stared at her, his face illuminated by moonlight. "You do not know what you are saying. You think this a jest, but it is not. I will not risk having another child. Not when I cannot even help the daughter I have now. No, nor risk letting any woman as close to me as I once let my first wife, Juliet! I will not fall pretty to such folly."

Tessa threw back the covers. "That's utter nonsense!" she said, not troubling to hide her exasperation. "What happened to Anna was an accident, and you *have* helped her a great deal. One of these days she will recover completely and speak. You will see."

"That is not what the experts have said when I consulted them."

Tessa made a rude noise and climbed out of the bed, ignoring the instinctive gesture Rivendale made to stop her. She swayed on her feet, but she would not be deterred. She took a step toward him.

"I do not care what anyone has said—they are mistaken! Anna will be fine! And so will you, if you will only allow yourself to risk loving again."

Now she was face-to-face with him, her forehead all but

touching his chin. She looked up at him. He, in turn, seemed to find great fascination in the locket at her throat and could not look away.

"I can't," he whispered.

In answer, she reached up to twine her arms around his neck and pull his face down so that she could kiss him. And just before she did, she, too, whispered. Only her words were, "You will, William."

It was a promise, a challenge, a gift. He wanted to resist, she could see it in his face. But instead he groaned, and then caught her up in as tight an embrace as she could have wished. And his lips closed over hers, demanding entrance. She granted it willingly.

She felt the moment William surrendered, and his hands began to roam over the body he had just begun to learn. It came as no surprise when he lifted her and carried her over to the bed. For a moment she feared he would find the resolution to walk away, but he did not. Instead, with another groan, he pulled off his robe and joined her. And repeated with her all the delights they had shared the night before. And in the midst of it, he even called her Tessa.

This time, when he would have left her bed to go to his own, she put her arm over his chest to stop him, and when he turned to protest, she kissed him. In the end William lay beside her all night long. They both slept more soundly than either had in some time. And that was how the servants found them in the morning.

The maid gave a little cry of astonishment, but even as Rivendale started to curse, the girl scurried back out of the room, muttering apologies. It was Tessa who noticed the small smile on the girl's face. She refrained, however, from telling William, for she was not certain if he would have been gratified or distressed.

Instead she said, gravely, "Is it such a terrible thing for the servants to know we are truly married? Will they not

have assumed such a thing? Or would you rather they spec-
ulated as to why we are not?"

That gave Rivendale pause, as she had hoped it would.
And she took the opportunity to be the first to leave the
bed. Let him think she was able to take all of this at least as
lightly as he did. He was not, after all, a man to be led but
rather one to be persuaded.

Behind her, Tessa could hear William getting to his feet,
grumbling as he looked for his robe. She found it on her
side of the bed and handed it to him, enjoying the way he
blushed over his lack of clothing.

And perhaps she handled the situation well, for before he
left the room, he came to stand behind her and placed his
hands on her shoulders. When she looked up inquiringly, he
bent forward and kissed her.

It was more than she expected. And if he did not follow
it with the words of love she would have liked to hear,
Tessa could not bring herself to complain. Instead, as he
stared at her, confusion evident in his expression, she
teased him yet again.

"Shall we wager," she asked mischievously, "on which
of us will be downstairs and ready for breakfast first? My
gown has an impossible number of buttons to be fastened,
but you will have to tie your cravat and I know how demanding an endeavor that can be."

Her words eased the tension, as she had hoped they
would. He tapped the tip of her nose and retorted, "I shall
engage to be first downstairs, though you have the unfair
advantage of already being in your own room."

She laughed and waited until he reached the doorway before she asked, "What shall we wager?"

William's eyes seemed to turn smoky as his thoughts
clearly mirrored hers. In a voice that was not altogether
steady he replied, "I am certain we shall think of something."

And then he was gone. Tessa moved swiftly to dress as

múch as she could on her own, knowing someone would be watching and send her maid in to her the moment Rivendale left the room. She was determined to win this wager, determined to be the one to name the forfeit. And if it was one that they both could enjoy, well, then, so much the better.

Sure enough, she was pulling a dress out of her wardrobe when her maid came into the room. "An extra tenpence, Dorothea," Tessa promised, "if you can get me gowned and my hair pinned up in half the time as usual!"

The other woman's eyes gleamed with speculation, and she hurried to do as she was bid. And Tessa suspected it was not just the promise of the reward that hurried her along.

Well, the gossip belowstairs would no doubt be very interesting today! And that could do William no harm. She had already realized they regarded him with affection and would be happy to see any change in his circumstances that promised to make him happier.

But as much as she hurried, Tessa reached the breakfast room at precisely the same moment as Rivendale. Under the approving and fatherly eye of his majordomo they both burst into laughter. It was, Tessa thought, a most auspicious beginning to the day.

Chapter 16

Tessa went up to the nursery later that morning. This time Anna looked at her, and when she realized there was no manuscript in her hands, turned her back once again. Nor would she let Tessa hold her today. And when she tried to talk to her, Anna clapped her hands over her ears and began to rock from side to side.

With a sigh, Tessa kissed the top of the child's head and left the nursery. Downstairs she found that Rivendale had again gone out. Restless, she went back to her room, where she found her maid clucking over the damage to the gown she had worn the night before to the theater.

"You'll not be able to wear it again," Dorothea said. "Not with the ribbon half ripped away and the stitching come undone as it has."

But Tessa could not agree. To be sure, she had not liked being shoved to the ground, but the memory of what happened after William brought her home ensured that she would always adore this dress. She quickly made a decision.

"I shall go and get a new ribbon to replace the old one," Tessa said. "You are quite right that it is not salvageable. But I am handy with a needle. I shall easily be able to repair the rest of the damage to the dress and then stitch the new ribbon into place. Merely cut me a bit of the old one. I shall match it if I can. If not, well, I am certain I can find something satisfactory."

Dorothea looked at her mistress doubtfully, but she did

as she was bid. Tessa tucked the bit of ribbon into her reticule, then said, "Please fetch my spencer and my bonnet. The sooner I go, the less crowded the shops will be."

The maid hesitated. "Should you be wishing me to go with you?"

Tessa started to agree, for she had a notion William would prefer that she not go alone. And Dorothea had lived in London all her life, so she would know the streets and shops better than Tessa. But something in the other woman's face made her ask, "Is there something you would rather do?"

"I had hoped to beg the day off," Dorothea admitted. "I've been sent word my mother is ill, you see, and I wanted to go and visit her."

"Of course you may have the day off," Tessa told her warmly. "Go and visit your mother. And ask Cook to give you some broth to take her."

For the first time since William had hired this intimidating woman to attend Tessa, she felt the maid approved of her. A broad smile lit Dorothea's face as she dipped a curtsey and said, "Thank you, ma'am. I'm right grateful, I am."

"Just go and see to your mother's health," Tessa said. "Take the entire day and don't worry about hurrying back. I shall manage, I promise you."

"I shall leave right after I fetch your spencer and bonnet," Dorothea said. "I shall also tell Giles to have the carriage brought around for you."

"No," Tessa said, making up her mind on the spot. "I shall walk."

"Walk?" the maid asked, clearly aghast.

"It cannot be above a mile or two, and I always feel better after a brisk walk."

Dorothea looked at Tessa doubtfully but she was too grateful for the favor granted to protest. "As you say. I'll get your things."

So it was that Tessa set out alone. She felt a moment's

qualm when Giles asked whether she wished perhaps to take a different maid or a footman with her. But in the end she refused.

"You must know I am accustomed to going out and about on my own," she told him gently.

"In the country, perhaps," Giles said with a sniff.

She merely smiled and assured him again that she would be fine. Then she resolutely went out the door. She needed to be alone, though she could not explain that to him. Back home, whenever she had been troubled about anything, Tessa would go for long walks on her own. Well, going out shopping alone here would have to do.

It was somewhat farther than she expected, and the streets were more crowded. But no one troubled Tessa, and she scarcely noticed whom she passed, except to stop, from time to time, to ask a passerby and make certain she was headed in the right direction.

She had forgotten how much she missed such walks, and now she took full pleasure in this one. To be sure, she rather thought she would hail a hackney to return home, but that was for later. Now she enjoyed the lovely day and the gentle breeze.

Eventually she reached the shop Dorothea had recommended. It was a matter of moments to discover the clerk could not match her ribbon, but they spent an agreeable quarter of an hour discussing other possibilities. In the end, Tessa carried away with her one she thought she liked much better.

It was as she was coming out of the shop that she thought she saw Miss Winsham. It seemed unlikely, but Tessa tried to catch up to the woman anyway to see. After that odd visit from Miss Winsham the day before, Tessa was far too concerned to ignore the possibility that the woman might be her aunt. And if it was Aunt Margaret, she wanted to know what was going on.

The streets and sidewalks were very crowded, and she

found herself growing more and more frustrated as people blocked her way. But then Tessa saw the woman turn down an alleyway and she hurried to follow.

When she reached the narrow byway, Tessa hesitated, but she thought she saw the woman ahead of her, and it looked more and more as though it was Aunt Margaret. So Tessa plunged forward. When she was halfway down the alleyway, a man suddenly appeared and grabbed the woman ahead of her. Tessa rushed forward to help.

"Stop! Let her go! Let her go right now!" Tessa cried out.

Startled, the man let go. The woman turned and came toward Tessa, but she managed only a few steps before he seized her again. By this time Tessa was close enough to see that it was indeed Aunt Margaret. And to both her anger and astonishment, she realized the man was the man from the theater, the night before.

"Let her go!"

"Run, Theresa! Get help!" Miss Winsham cried out.

Tessa hesitated. She knew it was unlikely that she could rescue her aunt alone, and yet she also knew that if she went back out to the street, by the time she found help, Aunt Margaret and the man would be long gone.

The man settled the matter. With his other hand, he reached out and grabbed Tessa's arm as well. "Meddling, are ye? Well, ye'll come along too!"

Margaret and Tessa were determined not to be taken easily, however. Tessa kicked out and felt her toe connect with the man's leg. Aunt Margaret landed a blow to the side of his head. A few more such blows and they began to think they might actually fight free.

Perhaps the man thought so too, for suddenly he let go of both women. But before they could run, he clouted them each so hard that they sank to the ground, their heads swimming.

Tessa fought to clear her senses. She reached out for Miss Winsham, thinking to grab her hand and pull her back down the alleyway. Perhaps if he saw how determined they were, he would let them go.

But it didn't work that way. Someone had heard the scuffle, but not the right someone. This person helped the first man seize both women, tie their hands behind them, and bind dirty rags into their mouths to keep them from screaming. And before Tessa could even think what to do, she and Aunt Margaret were bundled into a waiting hackney that blocked the other end of the alleyway.

Clearly it had been waiting for their captor, for the moment he had them lifted into the carriage and closed the door on the three of them, he tossed a coin to the person who had helped him, and the hackney pulled away.

Tessa struggled against her bonds, but they were tied much too securely. Nor could she push the gag out of her mouth. Beside her, Aunt Margaret moaned. All Tessa could do was look at her with worry and glare at their captor.

He gave a nasty laugh at that. "Don't be blaming me, Missy. 'Tweren't my notion to take you along of her. You're the one couldn't leave things alone! Last night you couldn't help but get in my way, aye, and got knocked down for your pains. She's the one what ought to of been taught a lesson. Then there'd have been no need for any of this today. But no, you had to meddle then and you had to meddle now. Well, far as I can see, Missy, anything happens to you is your own fault."

Miss Winsham moaned again and the man sighed. "Now look of what you made me do. 'Tweren't my plan to hurt her neither—leastwise not today. Last night t'were supposed to be that sort of warning, today was just supposed to be a simple snatching, it was. Wouldn't have that blow to her head, she wouldn't, if it weren't for your meddling, Missy. Dunno what me master and mistress will say. Bringing back two hens, when they asked fer one."

Then he leaned back against the cushions and closed his eyes. It wasn't a long ride, but Tessa took advantage of every moment to try to loosen the ropes tied around her wrists. She would have tried to see where they were going, but dark curtains covered every window.

When it became evident to Tessa that she could do nothing about the ropes binding her, she tried to feel for Miss Winsham's, thinking that perhaps she could manage to untie her. But their captor noticed and immediately pushed the two women apart.

"Here now, none of that!"

From that moment on, he kept his eyes wide open, staring from one to the other. Tessa gave up the fruitless attempt to undo her ropes and instead turned her thoughts to what they might do when the carriage stopped. She meant to take advantage of any opportunity.

As though he guessed her thoughts, their captor snorted and said, "Females! Can't accept what's done, can you? Well, wasting your time, you be. Won't be anyone allowing of you to escape. Worth their lives to help—or even look the other way. No, you'll be in me master and mistress's hands, and they won't let you go easily."

Tessa glanced over at Aunt Margaret and was relieved to see that this time her eyes were open. She gave a tiny prayer of thanks and looked anxiously to see if her aunt were still dazed. But Miss Winsham had recovered, it seemed, for she regarded Tessa with an apology in her eyes. And then she glanced obliquely at their captor.

Well, Tessa thought, feeling absurdly better, Aunt Margaret seemed to have recovered both her determination and her shrewdness. She could only hope it would be enough. And hope that an opportunity would present itself to use them. Meanwhile, though, perhaps it would be best if their captor thought them both thoroughly cowed.

To that end, Tessa tried to look frightened. She hunched back against the cushions and looked at the man with what she hoped was a terrified expression. Beside her, Aunt Margaret must have done the same, for the man chuckled.

"Aye, that's better. Understand your situation now, do you? Good! Dunno what's intended, but I'd hate to have to bash you both again. Better you accept you've gots no choices. Ah, here we be."

The hackney turned sharply into what Tessa thought must be a courtyard. Were they at an inn, then? she wondered. She wished she could draw back the curtains to see. But, in any event, the hackney did not stop. Instead it turned again, and then twice more, until finally it drew to a halt in what turned out to be another narrow alleyway. There was barely room to open the carriage door and squeeze out.

Hands were waiting to catch Tessa and Aunt Margaret, and they could smell water nearby. Were they on the docks? The notion terrified Tessa. What if their captors meant to send them away on a ship? At best they would find themselves impossibly far from home, and at worst they would be tossed overboard at sea.

But there was no time to think about such matters. Tessa had to focus all her attention on the cobblestones below her feet, or she would have fallen. Her captors were clearly eager to get them out of sight of the street. A door opened and they were shoved inside.

They were forced down some rickety steps and into a lighted room that must have been belowground. A musty, damp scent pervaded the place, and Tessa could not help but wrinkle her nose in disgust.

"Don't like the place, eh?" a woman asked, coming out of the shadows.

"Too fine for the likes of us?" the man at her shoulder demanded.

Then the woman turned to the man who had caught Tessa and Miss Winsham in the first place. "Why are there two of them?" she demanded. "We told you to fetch only the one."

He shuffled his feet and answered with a meekness at odds to any side of himself he had shown Tessa and Aunt

Margaret thus far. "'Tweren't my notion! This one saw me and tried to stop me from taking t'other."

"Why didn't you wait until she was alone?"

"I thought she were. Didn't have no one with her, for all the distance I followed before I tried for the snatch. But this one, she came from nowhere, I'll swear. She's the one what stopped me delivering the warning, last night. And now she got in me way again today. I had to bring her along or she'd have cried down a heap of trouble about me head."

There was a hint of desperation in his voice, and the woman sighed. "Very well. You did the best you could, I suppose. You may go."

"Me pay?"

"We shouldn't pay you anything for bungling matters so badly," the man retorted. "But here. Now go."

There was an edge to the man's voice that caused the other one to grab his coins and hastily retreat. That, more than anything else, told Tessa how dangerous the people holding them were. Best indeed to pretend to a meekness that might cause them to underestimate her, for given their captor's reaction, she had a notion that these two, the man and the woman, would not hesitate to rid themselves of anyone they considered a nuisance.

So Tessa kept herself in a huddled position and avoided looking directly at them. Instead, as though afraid to meet their gaze, she let her eyes flit anxiously around the room. The corners were in shadow, and she could see no other exit save the one through which they had entered.

But perhaps her acting was not as skilled as she hoped, for the man said, not troubling to hide his amusement, "Looking for a way to escape? There's only two ways out. The door through which you came, and the trapdoor in the corner that leads to the river below. And if you go out that way, you'll not be seen alive again. Now, shall we talk?"

Chapter 17

It was a measure of their self-assurance that the captors, a man and a woman, did not hesitate to remove the gags from Tessa and Miss Winsham's mouths, or to untie the ropes that bound their wrists.

"There really should have been no need for such a thing," the man said, an edge of humor to his voice. "We only wish to talk."

"Talk?" Miss Winsham asked defiantly. "Or do you mean threaten? I'll not stop rescuing children."

The man spread his hands wide. "But why should you care about such urchins? What can they mean to you? You are a lady—of sorts. Stay among your own class and leave us to ours," he ended with a growl.

Miss Winsham shook her head obstinately, and Tessa wanted to shake *her*. Didn't she realize the danger they were in, the man's soft words to the contrary?

Something must have drawn the woman's attention to Tessa, because she abruptly interrupted the man and said, "Wait! Before we say anything more, I should like to know who this person is, why she tried to interfere, and what her interest is in all of this."

The man nodded, conceding the point. "Excellent notion. Who are you? And why do you keep coming to her defense?"

"It was not my intent to do anything, last night," Tessa said, in an acid tone. "Your man ran into me, purely by accident. As for today, how could I have ignored any woman being attacked?"

"But who are you?" the woman demanded, peering closer.

Tessa hesitated. Which would be safer? To claim her rank as Lord Rivendale's wife and risk being held for ransom or worse, or to claim to be someone so unimportant they wouldn't care what happened to her?

Aunt Margaret took the matter out of her hands. "She's a very important lady, and there will be those looking for her. Best you blindfold her and take her someplace safe and let her go. If anything happens to her, her husband will not stop until he avenges her."

The man and woman looked Tessa up and down and laughed. Tessa felt herself color up. She knew her gown was ripped and covered with splatters of mud from fighting with the man in the alleyway. She did not, she knew, look very important at all. But still she drew herself up to her full height.

Before Tessa could speak, however, the woman said, "She can't be an important lady. She wouldn't have been out on her own, if she were. Would have been a footman or maid or such with her. Which there clearly wasn't or she wouldn't have been so easy to snatch."

"But she's some sort of lady," the man said, rubbing his chin.

The woman snorted. "One of them odd ones, like this one here, what comes and pokes their noses where they don't belong. No, I'll wager her own family is sick of her and might even be grateful that we took her off their hands."

The man nodded. "Foolish, that's what it be," he said to Tessa and Miss Winsham. "Purely foolish to try to lie to us. How do you expect us to negotiate with you, if we can't trust you to speak the truth?"

He paused and turned to the woman. "P'rhaps," he said,

his voice almost purring, "it would be a good notion to give these *ladies* a little time alone to think over their situation."

"Aye, a very good notion," the woman agreed. "But bring the lantern away with us. Do them good to spend a little time with the rats."

"Oh, no, I don't think we need go quite that far," the man protested.

"I do," she retorted. "Bring the lantern."

The man shrugged apologetically to Tessa and Miss Winsham. "I daresay there ain't that many rats down here, anyways," he said.

Neither Tessa nor her aunt replied. They used the last moments of light before the man and woman disappeared behind the door to look about them and move toward the table.

"If we sit on this," Tessa said in the dark, "any rats that are here will not be able to reach us."

"Excellent notion," Miss Winsham agreed. "I am glad to see you still have your wits about you, Theresa, though I must say that I wish you had not been so foolish as to get yourself caught."

"The feeling, my dear Aunt Margaret," Tessa said dryly, "is mutual."

"Yes, but I need to do what I do. You could very easily have gone for help instead of following me, trying to interfere, and getting yourself caught."

"Oh, I see. You thought I should simply walk away? Impossible! There would have been no time to go for help. He would have had you away before I even reached the street!" Tessa countered.

Silence. Then Miss Winsham sighed. "I suppose you are correct. And I—reluctantly, mind you—admit that I should have been disappointed if you had not shown such spirit. Can't abide milk-and-water chits! I thank heavens not a one of my nieces could be described as such."

Tessa laughed, despite the desperate circumstances in

which they found themselves. But then she turned serious again. "Did anyone know where you were going? Is anyone likely to know where to look?"

"No. What about you? Won't your coachman miss you and send someone to tell Lord Rivendale where he lost you?"

"I didn't bring a coachman," Tessa said, and it was her turn to be reluctant to admit the truth. "It was such a fine day that I walked."

Miss Winsham sighed. "So we really are in the suds. Did anyone at least know where you were going?"

"My maid, Dorothea."

"Good. She will at least be able to tell Rivendale where to begin to look for us."

"Not for a while," Tessa replied gloomily. "I gave her the day free to go and visit her sick mother. She will not be back until very late."

Miss Winsham cussed. When Tessa made an instinctive sound of protest, her aunt said tartly, "I am not about to change my ways just because I am obliged to play propriety to you girls. I will not bend to anyone's notions of what I ought to say, or what I ought to do. I never have and I never will. In any event, I am past the age of having to care about such things, and I hope that someday you will be too. And as far as I can see, which isn't very far in this darkness, our situation deserves some cursing."

"What are we going to do?" Tessa asked.

"Rescue ourselves, of course," her aunt replied promptly, "since we cannot count on anyone to do it for us. Now the question is, do we try the door we came through, or do we take the trapdoor down?"

"You mean the one that leads to the river?" Tessa asked with a shudder.

"Certainly I mean that one. Unless, of course, you spotted another one before they took the lamp away?"

"No, no, in fact I didn't even see where that one was,"

Tessa admitted. "And I cannot see what use it would be to us anyway. We cannot swim, and even if we could, our skirts would immediately become so heavy with water that they would drag us under."

Miss Winsham was silent for a moment. "I suppose you are right," she said reluctantly. "Besides, I am fairly certain I hear rustling. And that probably means the rats are all around us. Foolish as it is of me, I find myself sadly reluctant to risk stepping on one and getting bitten."

"I do not," Tessa said fervently, "find that a foolish fear. Not in the least!"

"Well," Miss Winsham said, "we cannot just sit here and do nothing!"

Across town, Lord Rivendale frowned at his majordomo. He had just returned from time spent with friends and he had thought he was in an excellent humor.

"What do you mean, Giles, that Lady Rivendale just went out? Didn't she say where she was going?" William demanded.

In a voice that was carefully devoid of emotion or judgment, and an expression to match, Giles replied, "No, sir, she did not."

"Well, did Lady Rivendale take her maid, at least? Or a footman?"

"No, sir. Lady Rivendale refused all such suggestions on my part."

William began to feel his temper rising. "Did she tell anyone where she was going?"

"I cannot say, sir. I did not think it my place to question the staff as to her ladyship's comings and goings," Giles replied austerely.

"No, of course not. Very well, please find Lady Rivendale's maid and have her come to me. Perhaps she knows where my wife went."

"Lady Rivendale's maid is not here," Giles replied. "She

left shortly after her ladyship did. She said that Lady
Rivendale had given her the day free to visit her sick
mother."

"When will she be back?" William asked, not troubling
to hide his exasperation.

"I cannot say, sir."

"Well, when she does return, send her in to me!"

And with that, Rivendale stalked off to his library.

It was absurd, foolish beyond permission, to react so
strongly to Theresa going out for a walk, William told himself sternly. No doubt she had encountered a friend, or one
of her sisters, and was simply enjoying a comfortable coze
in someone's parlor.

There was no reason to be angry with her. After all, he
had gone out and not told Theresa where he was going.
Why should he expect her to inform him of her activities?
It was foolish to react this way. No doubt Giles wondered if
he were altogether himself, questioning the poor fellow in
such a way. As though he thought Giles should have kept
Lady Rivendale a prisoner here or something. And yet,
William could not shake his sense of unease. Or the loneliness he felt at his wife's absence from the house. And that
disturbed him most of all.

He had meant it when he vowed to protect his heart. He
had meant it when he said he would not allow any woman
close ever again. But after last night he was beginning to
realize that he could not keep that vow.

William let himself whisper her name aloud, "Tessa."

For once he did not try to call her Theresa, not here, not
now. For it was *Tessa* who was already indispensable to his
happiness. He could not shield his heart from her, for she
had stolen it already, in some unguarded moment when he
wasn't looking.

He needed her. He looked forward to coming home and
finding her ready to listen to what he had to say. He liked
the way she disposed of nonsense with a few choice words

and laughed so easily at things he might be tempted to take far too seriously.

But more than anything else, William wanted her touch on his arm, the sweet way she smiled at him, the warmth and acceptance always in her eyes when she looked at him. He needed her belief in him when he could not believe in himself. And right now he wanted to fill his arms with her. He wanted to see if Tessa tasted as sweet when he kissed her today as he remembered from the night before.

And so, despite the fact that he knew it was foolish, William found himself pacing obsessively about the room. And as the day wore on, his sense of unease grew deeper. When he could stand the silence no longer, he went to see if perhaps she had gone to visit her sisters. That, after all, would not have been such a long walk from the house.

He ought not to have been surprised that Lady Stamford and her sister and aunt were out, but somehow he was. So he asked instead to speak with Sir Robert.

Stamford took one look at his face and offered him brandy. William waved it away. "More marriage troubles?" Sir Robert asked sympathetically.

"No," William said slowly. "At least I don't think so. It is just that my wife is not at home, and I don't know where she went. She did not take the carriage and she has been gone since this morning. I thought perhaps she had come here, to see her sisters, but apparently I was mistaken."

"I wonder," Stamford said thoughtfully, "if she could have gone somewhere with Miss Winsham. She also went out this morning and has not yet come home. And she did not go to pay morning calls with my wife and her sister! To be sure, Miss Winsham sometimes is gone all day and seems none the worse for it. But I've no notion where she goes, or what she does, for one doesn't quite like to ask her."

William nodded. "No, one would not want to question

Miss Winsham. One can guess she would demand how one had the temerity to do so!"

Stamford grinned. "Precisely!" He paused, and then said carefully, "Don't get angry at me, but I need to ask. Did you and Lady Rivendale quarrel? Is that why you are worried about her going out?"

William shook his head. "No, we parted after breakfast on the best of terms. At least I thought we did." It was his turn to hesitate before he said, "It did occur to me that perhaps she is not happy that I have been going out each day without telling her and that perhaps she is getting back a little of her own by doing this."

"There. A perfectly rational explanation. And just like Lady Rivendale," Stamford said heartily. "She does have a bit of a temper, you know."

"I know," William agreed. "And perhaps that is all this is. But I find myself unaccountably worried anyway."

"Well, I shall ask Alex and Lisbeth, when they return, if they have seen her today or knew her plans," Stamford said. "Perhaps they even stopped and took her up with them. Or, if you prefer, you may stay and ask them yourself, when they return. They should not be very late, for they are expecting several ladies to call upon them later this afternoon."

William shook his head. "No, I want to go back, in case Lady Rivendale has come home. Just send me word if they know anything."

"I shall."

Chapter 18

The man and woman glared at Tessa and Aunt Margaret. They began with the same question they had asked earlier. "Why must you muck about with urchins?"

"Why should you care if I do so?" Miss Winsham countered. "I have paid good money for the children I take."

"Because they're our business," the man growled. "Ours and friends of ours. A group of us, you might say, that Granny and I speak for. How are chimneys to be cleaned if you take away the climbing boys? And the girls what go to those houses, they're well taken care of. What else would they be doing, if they wasn't pleasing gentlemen?"

"Stop!" Miss Winsham said, her face betraying her revulsion. "You talk as if you are doing those girls a favor! Do you truly think so? Children of less than ten? None of whom, even the ones a little older, given a choice? Have you looked at their faces? Seen the terror? Or the climbing boys? Have you counted their burns? Or the bruises? And what about the beggar children on the street?"

"Good money was paid for them brats!" the woman spat at Miss Winsham. "You be taking the profits away from us. And how do you think *we* was raised?"

Unable to stay silent any longer, Tessa spoke up, her voice shaking with emotion. "All the more reason for you not to mistreat children, as you were mistreated. All the more reason for you to understand why it is wrong."

The man gave a snort of disgust. The woman seemed to

grow even more enraged. "What do you know of any of this? You, with your soft bed at night? What do you know of choices the likes of us must make?"

"Enough to want to make sure the children we help never have to make the same choices," Miss Winsham answered, her voice steady but determined.

"Ah! Foolishness! You can't save all the children!"

"We can save some."

"A bare handful," the man said coaxingly. "What's the point to that?"

"If it's so few," Tessa asked, "then why do you object? You've said yourself there are plenty of others to choose from. So why object if she rescues a handful or two? Especially since, as she has said, she pays good money for the children."

"Because it sets a bad example, that's why," the man growled.

"Gives the others notions," the woman added angrily. "They starts talking about the lady what will spirit them away, and then you can't get no work out of 'em at all."

"What a pity," Miss Winsham said, not bothering to hide the sarcasm in her voice.

"A pity for you. For the both of you," he warned. "We're not about to let you change the way things are."

"You cannot stop us," Miss Winsham said. "Oh, I've no doubt you can dispose of me, if you choose. But I am not the only one who is concerned. There are others funding me and helping me locate children to rescue. If you stop me, someone will take my place."

It was plain that this was not what the couple wanted or expected to hear. They looked at one another, obviously bewildered that neither Tessa nor Miss Winsham had been cowed by anything they said, or by the time spent down here in the dark.

Finally the man gave up. He turned to the woman and

said, "Let's see what they say in the morning, after they've spent a night down here, damp and cold and hungry!"

"You cannot starve us," Miss Winsham said firmly.

"Why not?"

"It wouldn't be proper!"

The pair were still laughing over that one as they locked Miss Winsham and Tessa in again. The room was once more pitch-dark.

"It wouldn't be proper?" Tessa echoed in disbelief.

Her aunt's voice was reassuringly calm as she replied, "It is always wise to have one's enemies conclude one is a fool. They are then much more likely to make mistakes. And since it was evident that they were going to lock us in here without food no matter what we said, there could be no harm in pretending to be an old woman in her dotage."

"You are not," Tessa said dryly, "so very old as that! You might get away with such a masquerade when you lived in your cottage in the woods and dressed as you wished, but here in London, properly gowned, you are far younger than my sisters or I ever realized."

"Well, in any event," Miss Winsham countered, "let them think me foolish. They may not bother to check on us tonight if they do."

"And how will that help us?" Tessa asked doubtfully.

"Why, because we are going to escape, of course!" Miss Winsham replied, as though it were self-evident.

"Oh, naturally. And of course you have a plan?"

"Well, I have a lock pick in my reticule and means to pin up our skirts if we decide to go down through the trapdoor that leads to the river."

Tessa decided that perhaps she didn't want to ask her aunt any more such questions. Instead she asked, "Maybe we should have told them who I am. Perhaps it would have made them think twice about abusing us in such a way."

"Perhaps," Miss Winsham said, "but I have been thinking and I realized that it would not be wise. That, indeed, it was a mistake on my part, the first time, to try to tell them you were in any way important."

"Why?" Tessa demanded. "Shouldn't it have made them afraid to harm us?"

Her aunt shook her head. "I realized that if they did realize you were Lady Rivendale and that I had the support of Sir Robert, it would not help us. I realized that it was far more likely that they would decide they must put paid to our existence, for we have seen their faces and could betray them in court. If they knew you were Lady Rivendale, then they would know that your husband had the resources to send Bow Street Runners to find them, and then to pay for a prosecution. As would Sir Robert. I am afraid they might feel they had to kill us. No, I am persuaded it is better to let them think that we are both simply shabby genteel ladies. Persons of no importance whatsoever—as they already believe me to be. I am persuaded it is wiser to let them think that neither of us has the resources to pursue them if we escape."

Tessa had no answer to that. While she was pondering the situation, Miss Winsham began to explain what she intended for them to do.

"We shall wait a good quarter of an hour. Just in case our captors are waiting to see if we try to escape by the door. Then we shall try to pick the lock. If we do succeed in getting out, we shall want to look like ladies of the docks, so as not to draw attention to ourselves."

Diverted, Tessa asked, "But I thought they did try to draw attention to themselves."

"Well, yes, but I mean we do not wish to appear as though we do not belong. And our best disguise is to dress like them. They will naturally take exception to us invading their territory and chase us off."

"Naturally," Tessa murmured. "It sounds positively delightful."

"Well, you know, we want anyone watching to think it is

merely a dispute between doxies and not to wonder if they ought to stop us from leaving. As they might, if they did not already assume they knew what was going on. It is, after all, the sort of thing that happens all the time down here."

"I did not know you were such an expert on the matter," Tessa said faintly.

Miss Winsham snorted. "I am not a fool. I made it my business to learn about every area I meant to go into to find the children. And I made it a point to befriend women in all these places. If we are fortunate, we will see one of them here, and she will help us."

"I see."

And, Tessa thought soberly, she did. It was unconventional, and no other woman she knew would even have thought of such a thing. But as Aunt Margaret so often said, she *was* an unconventional woman.

"What do we need to do?" Tessa asked.

"Once we are outside, we shall have to lower the neck-lines of our dresses—and you will have to discard your spencer. Perhaps we should even tear our dresses in a spot or two, so that they look well worn. But for now, I think perhaps it is time to make our way over to the door."

"What about the rats?"

"Bother the rats! We've more important things to think and worry about than them!"

William stood in his wife's bedroom. It was time to dress for dinner, and still she was not home. Nor was her maid. He felt a mounting frustration, and a growing certainty that something was very wrong. Perhaps, he thought, she might have mentioned something to Anna or Nanny.

He took the stairs two at a time, wishing he had thought of this possibility earlier. But when he asked, Nanny shook her head.

"No, sir. Her ladyship said not a word of what her plans might be."

"Did she read to Anna?"

"No, and when the child saw that she was not holding a manuscript she refused to even look at her. Lady Rivendale left the nursery looking so discouraged that it near broke my heart, sir."

A small hand tugged at William's arm. He looked down to see Anna staring up at him and looking worried. "Did you hear Lady Rivendale say anything about where she meant to go?" he asked his daughter, though he did not think it likely.

Anna shook her head. He turned to go, and she grabbed his arm again. She looked, he thought, as if she were going to burst into tears at any moment.

"Are you worried about her?" he asked.

Anna nodded, and William felt as though he had a lump in his throat. So his angry little daughter did care. He lifted her up and hugged her tightly.

"She will be back," he said, with a certainty he did not feel.

He set Anna down again and beat a hasty retreat from the nursery. Downstairs, he asked Giles yet again about his wife's maid.

"No, sir, she has not yet returned. Shall I ask Cook to set back dinner?" he asked.

Rivendale hesitated. "Yes. Perhaps an hour."

"Yes, sir."

William knew he was creating chaos in the kitchens with this order and that Cook would no doubt threaten to quit over the meal probably being ruined. But he had no appetite, and he could not imagine eating without Tessa. Somehow she had become necessary to him. Not to know where she was worried him more than he would have guessed.

When the hour had passed, William forced himself to sit down to dinner. But it was with a very diminished appetite, and only the thought that he would do neither himself nor

Tessa any good by starving persuaded him to swallow anything at all. Still, he was relieved when the last of the dishes
was taken away, and he refused the brandy Giles would
have poured for him.

"Sir?" Giles asked, clearly taken aback.

"My wife is missing. I do not believe it is something she
would do of her own choice. I choose, therefore, to keep a
clear head about me tonight."

"Very good, sir."

It was evident that Giles did not share William's certainty about the matter, but then Giles had not shared her
bed or her laughter, or heard her words of love.

Even as Rivendale was heading toward his library, the
knocker on the front door sounded. He paused where he
was to see whom Giles would admit. It was Stamford.
William felt his hopes dashed yet again. Still, he was polite
as he called down to Giles not to refuse him entrance, but
rather to show Sir Robert straight upstairs.

When they were alone in the library, Stamford came
straight to the point. "Miss Winsham has not returned
home. I gather from your expression that your wife has not
returned either."

"No."

"Then I think, Rivendale, we must consider the possibility that something has happened to one or both of them.
Since I do not believe in coincidence I must also guess they
are together. I have come to see whether anything has yet
occurred to you as to where to look?"

"I wish that it had," William said heavily. "I have tried
and tried to think, but I have not the least notion."

Just then there was a rapping at the library door and
Giles opened it far enough to poke in his head and say, "I
am sorry to disturb you, sir, but Lady Rivendale's maid has
returned. Shall I ask her to wait until after Sir Robert has
left to come in to speak with you?"

"No!" The two men spoke as one and it was William

who added, "Send Dorothea in at once. Sir Robert may wish to hear what she has to say as well."

"Yes, sir."

Within minutes the rather frightened maid was standing trembling in front of the two men. William tried to set her at ease.

"It's all right, Dorothea. We know that Lady Rivendale gave you leave to visit your mother, and that is perfectly all right. I am not angry. I merely wished to ask you whether you have any notion where Lady Rivendale meant to go when she left the house this morning."

"Just out to buy some ribbon, sir. To replace the one that was torn on her gown last night," Dorothea said with some bewilderment.

"She couldn't have," William objected. "She didn't have the carriage sent 'round."

"She said she wanted to walk, sir. Said she missed it from when she was back home," Dorothea explained. "I tried to tell her it was too far, but she wouldn't heed me. But even walking she ought to have been back long ago, shouldn't she, sir?"

"We think so," Rivendale said grimly. "Did she mention meeting anyone? Perhaps Miss Winsham?"

Dorothea shook her head. "Not a word to me, sir."

"I see. Thank you, Dorothea. You may go. Oh, and how is your mother?"

Dorothea blinked back a tear. "Much better, sir. And I was that happy coming back tonight, thinking it was good news I could give her ladyship about my mother. Only to find she'd gone missing and not come home yet."

"Try not to worry," William said awkwardly. "We shall find her."

The woman nodded and left the library. The two men stared at one another grimly. "A ribbon," Stamford said slowly. "That gives us some notion of where your wife went. And we shall presume she took Miss Winsham with her or met her on the way. It is, at any rate, a place to start."

"But not," William said with patent frustration, "until tomorrow morning! No one will be at any shop at this hour. And in any event, it is more likely it would have been someone on the street who saw where they went." He paused, then added, "Why the devil couldn't she have taken the carriage? At least then perhaps my coachman would have seen something!"

Stamford grimaced. "I suppose for the same reason Miss Winsham apparently walked to where she could hail a hackney. They are far too independent, the pair of them. And I haven't a notion how to cure them of it, except that perhaps this misadventure will do so."

But they both shared the same unspoken thought: If the two women came back at all.

It was William who tried to shake off the grim mood. "This is absurd!" he said. "What could happen to two ladies such as Lady Rivendale and Miss Winsham?"

Stamford looked at him with eyes that held far too much knowledge. "You don't want to know," he said softly. At Rivendale's look of inquiry, he added reluctantly, "This would not be the first time Miss Winsham has placed herself in harm's way. Over a child, I should venture to guess."

"In that event we ought not to wait for morning!" William said with some alarm.

"If you could suggest where we ought to begin, I should be glad to oblige you," Stamford replied.

From the doorway of the library, a voice drawled, "Perhaps I can help?"

"Kepley!"

William could not help the exclamation, but then he halted, uncertain what to say. Even to his very good friend, he was reluctant to admit that Theresa was missing. "What the devil are you doing here?" he asked weakly.

Kepley came into the room and carefully closed the door

behind him. "I presume you forgot your appointment to meet me at the club tonight."

William colored up. "Er, yes. I had other things on my mind."

"So I overheard. Not intentionally, I assure you. But the library door was not completely closed," Kepley said. "And perhaps it is just as well, because I may be able to help. I can, at the very least, tell you where I saw Lady Rivendale this morning."

"Never mind telling us," William said impatiently. "Will you show us?"

"Of course."

They looked at Stamford. "Oh, very well," he said. "Why not? By all means let Kepley show us where he last saw Lady Rivendale. And let us also call the maid back in here and ask her the precise shop where Lady Rivendale meant to go. We will no doubt find nothing of use, but at least we can try."

William nodded and moved toward the library door. Over his shoulder he said, "It will be faster if we go in search of Dorothea ourselves and ask her. I presume you have your carriage waiting outside."

"Of course."

"Good."

It was a only matter of minutes to find Dorothea in the kitchens. The entire staff scattered as William and Stamford and Kepley invaded their domain, but none of the men cared. All that mattered was that Lady Rivendale had discussed shops with her maid. And Dorothea might be able to tell them where to pursue their search if Kepley's starting point failed them.

And then they were on their way.

Chapter 19

As it turned out, the street where Kepley had seen Lady Rivendale walking was the same street where the ribbon shop was. It was a lowering thought to realize he could tell them no more than had Tessa's maid.

Still, there was a full moon tonight, a circumstance for which the three men were grateful. It meant that not only could the coachman see where he was going, and they could see about them when they got out at the street of dry goods, but there were more people out walking around than would otherwise have been the case.

Mind you, no one admitted to having seen anything. Indeed, no one even admitted to having been there, on that street, earlier in the day when Tessa and Miss Winsham had been there. Rivendale, Kepley, and Stamford conferred briefly.

"The more I think of it," Kepley said slowly, "the more I think I saw Lady Rivendale turn into one of the alleyways. I didn't think anything of it at the time, because I was talking with a friend as we rode by in his carriage and my leg was giving me the deuce of a time. But, yes, I think perhaps she turned into one of the alleyways."

"Yes, but which one?" Stamford asked.

Kepley shrugged. "I don't know. I wish I did."

"We'll explore all the alleyways," William said briskly. "I know we're not likely to find anything useful, but perhaps we'll be lucky. In any event, we have to try."

The other two nodded, and all three began to examine the alleyways, each taking a different one so as to cover the most ground as quickly as possible.

It was William who found the first clue. It was down an alleyway that he almost missed. He had determined to turn back when he noticed something glinting in the dark. When he moved closer, he realized that it was his wife's locket. He knelt down and picked up the intricately carved piece of jewelry. There could be no mistake, he thought. The locket was definitely hers.

Later he could not have said how long he knelt there, staring at the locket in his hand. It felt like an eternity, but it may have been only a few moments. In any event, it was long enough for Stamford and Kepley to come looking and find him there. William showed them his discovery.

"Alex's locket!" Stamford exclaimed.

"No, it belongs to my wife," Rivendale corrected him. "She has worn it ever since I have known her. I found it here on the ground."

"Perhaps the clasp gave way?" Kepley suggested.

William shook his head. "The chain is broken, but not at the clasp. I should guess there was a struggle and it was torn from her neck and fell unnoticed to the ground."

"Yes, but even if you are right, what the devil was she doing in this alleyway?" Stamford demanded.

"And where did she go from here?" Kepley added.

They looked around, and William suggested, "Through one of these doorways, perhaps?"

Stamford shook his head. He was studying the filth on the ground, grateful for the moonlight, though little enough penetrated into the alleyway. Still, it was more light than they would have had on any other night.

"I think not," he said. "Look here. You can see footprints in the muck. There were two ladies, and a man, I think, which means Miss Winsham may have been with Lady Rivendale, after all. I think they must have gone on down the alleyway. Let us see where it leads, and whether there continue to be signs they passed this way."

They came out onto another street, a cleaner one than the alleyway. William stared about him in frustration. "Now what are we to do? How can we possibly guess where they went from here?"

"A carriage stood waiting here, probably for some time. Perhaps waiting for whoever struggled with your wife and Miss Winsham," Stamford said, staring at a large pile of horse dung in the street.

"But why? And how would he know she would come this way?" William asked with pardonable exasperation.

"We cannot know the answers to that until we find them," Kepley said thoughtfully. "And I suggest we waste no time in doing so."

"Yes, well, I should like some suggestions of how we are to do that!" Stamford said sharply.

Rivendale looked at Sir Robert and grinned. "It seems to me," he said slowly, "that my wife said something about you having some rather, shall we say, unusual connections. Perhaps you might know someone who could help?"

Stamford hesitated and Kepley added, "For that matter, you and I, Rivendale, did enough clandestine enterprises when we were in school together, making forays into enemy territory to retrieve our property and such, that we are not precisely novices at this sort of thing ourselves. The stakes are just a bit higher this time around."

William nodded. To Sir Robert he said, "Well? Do you know anyone who could help?"

Stamford grimaced. "Perhaps, but it would take time to find such a person. Unless, perhaps if we went straight to Bow Street. I know a Runner or two who might have heard something or be able to help look for Lady Rivendale and Miss Winsham. At the very least, it's worth trying."

"Then why are we still standing here?" Kepley asked. "Let us go back to the carriage and go there straightaway!"

It might be late, but Bow Street did not close its doors. Certainly not to men like Sir Robert or Lord Rivendale or a war hero like Lord Thomas Kepley. And the Runner who listened to their story seemed earnest enough to please all three of them. Especially since it was clear Stamford had worked with the man before and trusted him.

"Now, first, why do you say someone would be wanting to abduct Lady Rivendale or Miss Winsham?" the Runner asked. "Ransom, do you think? Or someone wif a grudge against one of you gen'lemun?"

Stamford shook his head. "No. I believe Miss Winsham may have been trying to rescue children. Children whom she felt were being mistreated, as apprentices or in brothels or on the street."

The Runner stroked his chin. "Aye, that would have been enough to make any number of people angry," he agreed. "And them is not the sort to scruple against offering violence to a lady, I'll be bound. 'Deed, there's been rumors, there has, this past week, down by the docks, about a lady going about and mucking up trouble."

"Only one lady?" William asked sharply.

"Only one."

"Have there been rumors about plans for revenge?" Kepley chimed in.

The Runner hesitated. "They'd not have said so to the likes of me. But I'd be much surprised if they wasn't planning sumfing."

"Then we should go down to the docks and try to find them," William exclaimed, rising to his feet, impatient at the slow pace of the conversation.

Stamford put out a hand to stop him. "Wait. We cannot go there without a plan. It will do Miss Winsham and Lady Rivendale no good for us to be bashed on the head, either."

"And if they guesses some'un has come to find 'em," the Runner warned, "the ladies will disappear so thoroughly that we'll never find 'em. No, 'is nibs is right. We need a plan afore we go there. What does yer nibs suggest?" the Runner asked Stamford respectfully.

But it was William who answered. "I do have a plan," he said impatiently. And then, in a low voice, he began to explain.

Miss Winsham worked at the lock on the door. It would not budge.

"I thought you said you knew how to use the lock pick," Tessa whispered.

"I do, but not in the dark," Miss Winsham snapped. "Do you wish to try?"

"No, no, you go ahead," was the hasty reply.

"Then be quiet and let me do so!"

At the same moment they heard the voices. They were coming closer. Both women poised to move away from the door, or should that seem better odds, to try to push past the persons, if they opened the door.

But whoever it was apparently just wished to stand outside the door and talk. When it became evident that they were not going to move away anytime soon, Tessa and Miss Winsham retreated to where they could speak freely without risking being overheard.

"It will have to be the trapdoor," Miss Winsham said decisively.

"But he said it leads to the river!" Tessa protested. "And I cannot swim, though no doubt you will tell me you do, Aunt Margaret," she added with an edge to her voice.

"Well, yes, but I do not think it will come to that," Miss Winsham said soothingly.

"Why not?"

"Because, my dear, our captors are not fools. And while they might simply have put a trapdoor into the floor for a convenient way to dispose of unwanted persons, the odds are far greater that they also planned it as a means of escape, should they need another way out of the building."

"Oh, to be sure," Tessa said. "My goodness, Aunt Margaret, I had no notion you were so well informed as to the habits of people like these."

The older woman made a rude sound. "Quiet," she said. "Once we open the trapdoor that is what you must do—be quiet. Sound travels far too well over water, and we do not wish to be overheard making our escape. Now come along. Do you remember where the trapdoor was?"

It took some time to locate the thing in the darkness. Finally they found it by the sound of lapping water below. "I told you it led to the river!" Tessa said when they were both crouched over the spot.

"Hush! Help me open it and let me go first."

"I promise you, Aunt Margaret, I shouldn't dream of arguing with you over that!"

But despite her grumbling words, Tessa did as she was bid. And though it took a moment or two, they soon had the trapdoor open. The sound of rushing water was far stronger now, and Tessa could see nothing between the open hole in the floor and the water below.

Miss Winsham, however, ignored the water and seemed to be feeling about under the edges of the opening. After some moments she gave a tiny sound of delight.

"It is here!" she whispered.

"What is here?" Tessa asked, careful to pitch her voice just as quiet as her aunt had done.

"A rope ladder. If I am right, it will lead to strong netting attached to the underside of a pier. We can climb along that and get to shore."

"Oh, to be sure. Nothing easier in these skirts!" Tessa said dryly.

"We shall have to tie up our skirts, of course," Miss Winsham said tartly. "Here, help me close the trapdoor. It allows in no light anyway, and with it closed we need not be so quiet."

As Aunt Margaret helped her tie up her clothing so that it

would not impair what needed to be done, it occurred to Tessa that her aunt was far too practiced in what she was doing. How many times, she wondered, had the older woman done such a thing? And for what purpose had she done it? Surely she did not make a habit of getting captured and made prisoner above a river?

Still, for the moment Tessa was grateful for her aunt's expertise. It argued that perhaps they had a chance of escaping after all. She listened as the older woman explained what she thought they might face and how to deal with it. She listened as though her life depended on it, for she thought perhaps it did.

Eventually they were ready. Together they opened the trapdoor again. "I shall go first," Miss Winsham said, and then before Tessa could answer, she carefully went, feet first, over the edge.

Tessa put her hand on the top of the rope ladder as her aunt had told her to do. It alarmed her to feel the way it swayed as her aunt moved down the ladder. It was worse when the ladder seemed to suddenly swing back and forth. Was Aunt Margaret all right? she wondered.

At last she felt the tug on the ladder that her aunt had told her to expect. Her turn. Tessa took a deep breath, and as Miss Winsham had done, she carefully eased herself onto her stomach and felt with her feet for the rungs of the ladder.

It was not easy climbing down. The rope swayed with every movement she made. Still, she made herself go far enough down that she could pull the trapdoor shut over her head, just as Aunt Margaret had instructed her to do. And then she made herself keep going again, one rung at a time, until suddenly someone put a hand on her ankle.

Tessa started, but the hand stayed firm and she realized it must be her aunt. A moment later the other woman's voice confirmed it.

"All right. Now I must bring the ladder toward me. You

will feel more precarious than ever. But you are completely safe, so long as you do not let go. When I bring the ladder to me, you will have to twist around, reach for the net, and slide onto it. It feels fragile, but it will easily hold your weight, as well as mine."

"How can you be so sure?"

"Have we any other choice but to trust it?"

Tessa began to wish she had not asked. She began to wish even more that she had not descended this appalling ladder, as Aunt Margaret began to pull the bottom of it toward her.

It was not such a very great distance, but it was enough to incline Tessa at an angle that made her feel distinctly ill. Still, she held on tight. And when Aunt Margaret began to twist the ladder, Tessa reached out for the net her aunt had promised would be there. She clambered over onto it as quickly as she could, and laid flat on the netting, trying to catch her breath and calm her racing heart.

"Excellent. Now I shall tie this end of the ladder to the net. That way, if someone looks through the trapdoor, the ladder will be out of sight, just as if it was not there at all, or was still tied up under the door. Just as they must have planned to do themselves, if they came this way," Miss Winsham said in disgustingly cheerful tones. "We are almost free. All we must do now is scramble over the netting until we get to the riverbank."

"Oh, to be sure, that will be nothing at all," Tessa whispered back.

Miss Winsham did not bother to reply. She merely began to make her way over the netting. With a tiny groan, Tessa followed.

It wasn't easy. Particularly not when her skirts began to come undone from the way Aunt Margaret had tied them up. But it could not be helped. Neither woman wanted to linger. And soon, though not quite soon enough for Tessa's comfort, they reached the muddy riverbank. Together they managed to clamber up it, though not without a great deal of effort.

They were careful to keep to the shadows, for the moonlight threatened to give them away. Miss Winsham helped Tessa rearrange her skirts again, and then she said, "Now we must make ourselves look like street women."

"How are we to do that?"

"Well, the mud will help. Now we must lower the neckline of our dresses. Toss your spencer into the river! We must look as if we want men to notice us," Miss Winsham replied.

Tessa heard the sound of fabric tearing. A moment later, she felt her aunt's hands tearing at the neckline of her own dress, and before she could protest, she had what might easily have passed as the gown of a woman of the streets.

"Now," Miss Winsham said briskly, "follow me. We must be well away from here before they discover we are gone."

And so, with a sway to her hips, the older woman stepped out of the shadows and began to saunter down the street. Feeling a trifle dazed, as if perhaps she had wandered into Bedlam, Tessa had no choice but to follow. Later, however, she promised herself grimly, she and Aunt Margaret were going to have a very long talk, and she suspected it was going to be a very interesting one.

Chapter 20

O nce they reached the docks, Rivendale, Stamford, Kepley, and the Bow Street Runner conferred briefly in the carriage, going over the plan one last time.

"You'll give your coachman orders to keep an eye out for Miss Winsham and Lady Rivendale," William said to Stamford. "And you and our friend, the Bow Street Runner, are to find his contacts and see what they may know. Meanwhile, Kepley and I will walk about, keeping our eyes open."

"And your wits about you," the Runner warned.

"Of course," William said. "And we meet back here in one hour. Are we agreed?"

The other men nodded. Within moments they were out of the carriage and the coachman was given his orders. The men paused to look about. The streets were fairly deserted, except for precisely the sort of folk that one would not want to meet on a dark night.

Lord Thomas Kepley smiled a wry smile. Softly he said to Rivendale, "Last time I was with you and I saw a group of people this unfriendly was back at school, when we were surrounded in that last raid of ours."

William nodded. He could not help thinking that if Theresa and Miss Winsham really were here, in this appalling part of town, how could they possibly be all right?

He must have asked the question aloud, for the Runner replied in soothing accents, "Now don't you worrit none,

Lord Rivendale. They may be fine. P'rhaps whomever took 'em only wanted to throw a scare into the lady what was meddling with the children."

"And perhaps they decided to dispense with her altogether!" William replied in acid tones.

"Now, sir, there's no call to be thinking such things just yet," the Runner said. "We've only just got here and haven't even begun to ask questions. Give us time, sir, give us time, afore you go fretting yourself in such a way."

"He's right," Stamford added. "They would have little to gain, and much to lose, if they harmed Miss Winsham or Lady Rivendale."

"Unless they were absolutely certain it could not be traced back to them! Don't coddle me, either of you," William said with some exasperation. "I know that they may be all right. But I also know they may not, and I see no value in pretending otherwise."

The other men exchanged speaking glances, but they ceased to argue. Instead Kepley asked the Runner, "What, precisely, should we be looking for?"

"Anything out of place. Anyone who looks as if they'd like to speak with us, but don't quite dare. Keep a sharp eye open for anyone who looks as if they might be eager to earn a coin or two by telling tales. And look for any trace of a struggle, though I think they'd have wiped anything of the sort away by now."

"They didn't in the alley," William pointed out.

The Runner nodded his acknowledgment. "Didn't have time, I'll be bound. That were a better part of town. Someone might have stopped 'em if they'd lingered. But here, well, who's to care?"

"We must hope someone does," Stamford said with some asperity, "or we shall learn nothing."

"On the contrary," the Runner corrected him, "we must hope for someone greedy enough to betray an otherwise comrade. But we're wasting time. We'd best be off."

They split into pairs and moved off down the street in opposite directions. William kept in mind the Runner's words. They were to look for anything out of place and anyone who might be greedy enough to betray a friend.

It was Kepley who spotted their first target. "Look over there," he said softly to Rivendale. "That woman. She looks hungry, and perhaps desperate enough to talk. And the advantage is, if anyone sees us talking to her, they'll think we're just negotiating her fee."

William nodded. "You're right, but it should be only one of us. Two speaking to her will draw too much attention. Wait here and I'll be right back."

"No." At Rivendale's look of surprise, Kepley smiled wryly. "Let me go and speak with her. I'll limp even more than usual and lurch about a bit, as though I were deep in my cups. So when I walk away it will look as if she could not stomach servicing a drunken cripple. If you walk away, everyone watching will wonder why."

Rivendale didn't like it, but he had to admit his friend's words made sense. "All right," he said and stepped back into the shadows, the better to watch both his friend and anyone else who might be on the street.

From where William stood, it looked precisely like the sort of encounter Kepley had said it would. In the end, he made it look as if he had changed his mind, or more likely, as if she had decided she did not want him for a customer.

Kepley reeled back across the street. When he reached Rivendale he stood with one hand braced against the wall, still pretending to be three sheets to the wind as he told William what he had learned. Which was very little.

"There's a pair, a man and a woman, that have been making threats about a lady meddling in this part of town. She has a string of girls, and he a string of climbing boys and beggars and worse. No one took them seriously, though enemies of theirs have been known to disappear before. But no one believes they would actually dare harm a lady," Kepley said.

"Did she say where this pair might be found?" William asked.

"At a tavern down the next street over. At least that's where the woman is said to conduct some of her business," Kepley said grimly.

"And the man?"

"She said she didn't know. Perhaps she doesn't."

"Then the tavern it is," William said decisively.

They moved off down the street, never noticing that another man, Larkin, stepped up to the girl and began to question her. They had already turned the corner and were out of sight when the man slapped her.

Larkin hurried to catch up with the two who were so out of place in this part of town. He, on the contrary, clearly belonged. The few people out on the street knew him by sight and gave him a very wide berth.

Indeed, so well known was Larkin that all eyes were on him and no one noticed the girl slip away in the opposite direction. Nor would they have cared if they had. She was unimportant, a street drab, and there were too many of them in this part of town. Still, she kept to the shadows as she went, and hid the side of her face the man had struck. Street drab or not, she had her pride.

Tessa was cursing silently to herself, borrowing as many of Aunt Margaret's words as she could remember, as she slipped on the wet and muddy cobblestones. Beside her, Miss Winsham moved with the surefootedness of a mountain goat.

Their disguise must have been effective, for more than one man accosted them, thinking to buy their favors. Aunt Margaret dispensed with each fellow with a few coarse words that made him laugh and move away.

They hadn't gotten far, however, when a woman stepped

into her path. She had eyes that looked haunted and she was holding a hand over one side of her face. She looked to the sides and over her shoulder, as if to make certain no one was close enough to overhear. And then she spoke.

"Are you the two ladies them gen'lemun is looking fer?" she demanded, reaching out to grasp Miss Winsham's wrist.

"Ladies? Us? Hah!" Aunt Margaret laughed and pulled away.

"I'm trying to help you," the girl said, for she was a girl still. "There's two men, gen'lemun, asking fer two ladies, one younger, one older. One of 'em said the ladies was kidnapped today, and one of 'em had been meddling about with children. And I've seen you doing that, meddling with children," she told Miss Winsham. "Please, if it's you, let me help. I know the way to where they left their carriage."

"Why should you want to help us?" Tessa asked with a frown.

"'Cuz I wish someone had helped me, when I was a child!" the girl said, lifting her hand away from her cheek to show the bruise that was already forming there. "And 'cuz it ain't safe fer me to stay 'ere no more."

Tessa gasped in dismay. Miss Winsham clucked her tongue disapprovingly. Then, in a gentle voice she said, "You are still a child. And if you help us to get out of here, you may come with us. I shall undertake to get you out of the city, to a place where you may be safe, and you need never sell your body again."

The girl's eyes widened with surprise, and then something came into her eyes that was perhaps hope. "This way," she urged, still looking about to make certain no one was paying them undue attention. "It's only a few streets over that they left their carriage."

The coach was waiting just where the girl had said it would be. At the sight of what looked to be three street drabs approaching, however, the coachman leaned toward them and said, "Off with you! I'm on duty and don't want nor need company. Off with you, I said."

But by now they were close enough for the moonlight to show their faces to the coachman, and he gasped. "Miss Winsham? Lady Rivendale?" he asked, horrified.

"Yes, and we are very glad to see you," Tessa said. "This girl said some men were looking for us."

"Lord Rivendale, Lord Thomas Kepley, Sir Robert, and a Bow Street Runner," the coachman confirmed.

"We must go and find them and tell them we are all right," Miss Winsham said briskly.

"No!" the coachman exclaimed. "That is to say, it's as much as me job would be worth to let you go off again, now that you're found. Why don't you wait in the carriage? I'm certain they'll be back any moment." Miss Winsham hesitated, and he added, "Like as not, you'd only put them in more danger if you was to go looking for them now. They should be back at any moment."

"Very well," Miss Winsham said crossly. "We'll wait inside the carriage. But no more than a quarter of an hour, mind. After that, we'll go in search of Sir Robert and Lord Rivendale and Lord Thomas Kepley and the Runner."

"Yes, ma'am," the coachman said meekly.

His meekness, however, lasted only so long as it took for the three women to climb into the carriage and close the door behind them. The moment he judged them to be safely settled on the seats, he set off at the briskest pace he dared risk. Those were the orders Lord Rivendale had given him, and that was what he knew Sir Robert would also want him to do!

He would return for his master the moment he had them safely home, of course, but for now the coachman wasn't taking any chances. Not with the sorts he'd seen hanging about, he wasn't! Why, right over there was one of 'em, staring in a way that didn't look right. No, he weren't about to hang around here with the ladies, risking their safety and his.

Inside the coach, Miss Winsham began to sputter. If she could have thought of a way to do it, she would have thumped on the roof of the carriage and demanded that the coachman turn straight about. Tessa was no happier than her aunt.

"What will they think when they come back to find their carriage missing?" she demanded. "What if they need it? We ought to go back."

Only the third woman was sanguine. "I think we're well outer there. You can send the coach back, arter we get to some place safe."

Miss Winsham continued to grumble, but acknowledged the truth of what the girl had said. "I suppose you are right. Oh, very well. What we cannot mend we must accept. Now, tell me your name, child."

"Mary, ma'am."

"I see. Well, Mary, what talents have you, other than the obvious?"

"Dunno. I used ter take care of me mum, afore she died," Mary said doubtfully. "Taught me ter sew, she did, afore 'er eyes failed."

"Why didn't you become a seamstress then?" Aunt Margaret asked briskly.

The girl snorted. "Me? Wif no one ter speak fer me? Nor me able to talk flash fer the customers? Not likely."

"I see. But did you like to sew?"

"I s'pose."

Aunt Margaret leaned forward and patted the girl's hand. "Well, we shall see. I am going to send you to a place far away from London. There are other children there, and the people taking care of them will help you discover what you might like to do."

Mary looked a trifle doubtful, but she didn't object. Privately Tessa wondered how long the girl would stay where

Aunt Margaret sent her. But it was not, after all, her concern. She only hoped that Sir Robert and William and Kepley and the Bow Street Runner were safe.

She reached up to touch the locket at her throat, and that was when she realized it was missing. She gave a tiny cry of dismay.

"What's wrong?" Miss Winsham demanded.

"My locket! It's gone!"

Miss Winsham gaped at her niece. "That locket never goes missing," she muttered. "Not before it is time, at any rate. It's simply not possible."

"Yes, well, it is missing," Tessa retorted tartly. "And I have no notion when or how!"

"It will undoubtedly turn up again," the older woman said with conviction. "It must. And it will do so when it is most needed."

Tessa opened her mouth to argue, and then closed it again. If Aunt Margaret wished to cling to her illusions, what affair, after all, was it of hers? So she stared out into the street at the passing houses and wondered if anyone in any of them had ever had such an adventure as she and Aunt Margaret had shared today.

The carriage pulled to a halt in front of Sir Robert's town house, and a footman helped them all descend from the coach.

"What about Sir Robert? And Lord Rivendale? And Lord Thomas Kepley? And the Runner?" Tessa asked.

"I'll go back and fetch them straightaway, Lady Rivendale," the coachman replied.

She nodded and followed the others up the steps. The door was open, and Alex and Lisbeth stood there waiting to embrace them. Mary drew back a little, but Miss Winsham made her come forward and be introduced.

One of the maids was promptly summoned to take Mary down to the kitchen, where she might be given something to eat and then a bath and change of clothes. Mary looked a trifle alarmed at the latter prospect, but she was given no chance to object or to change her mind about being here.

The other ladies went upstairs toward the drawing room, for as Lisbeth said, "We want to hear every detail of what happened! Including how you come to be returning in Stamford's carriage without him."

"But first," Alex said, wrinkling up her nose, "the both of you need to wash and change. Tessa, I am certain I have a gown you may borrow, and I shall have my maid sent up to you straightaway. Aunt Margaret, I shall have Lisbeth's maid attend you. Yes, yes, I know you prefer to dress yourself, but this is one time I think you may need some assistance."

Chapter 21

The tavern was brightly lit and full of noise. Even so, eyes turned to study the two men who dared invade a place where they did not belong. Kepley continued his pretense of being three sheets to the wind.

William pretended to support him and muttered to those who seemed to look too close, "Soused! He'd just better not get sick on me. He hasn't the sense a babe was born with."

"Buy 'im a drink. If 'e passes out, you can take 'im 'ome and put 'im to bed," one onlooker suggested helpfully.

There were no free tables, so the two men made their way to the bar. There, Kepley demanded brandy. "The good kind, nothing watered down," he said, slurring his words convincingly. "M'leg hurts like the devil."

William laid the coins for the drinks on the bar. As he did so, he studied the faces in the room, looking for the woman the street drab had described to Kepley. He could also feel the hostility of those staring back. He wanted nothing so much as to be out of here. But he couldn't go. Not without Theresa and Miss Winsham. Not without making sure that no one here could help them.

Kepley must have seen something William didn't see, for suddenly he nudged Rivendale and whispered, "There. That table. C'mon."

Then, before William could ask what he meant to do, Kepley was reeling toward a particular table. It was a little off by itself, and others seemed to be giving it as wide a berth as they could—but not Kepley.

"Nurse!" he exclaimed to the woman sitting there. "What are you doing here?"

"What the devil?" her companion demanded, rising to his feet.

"Nurse?" the woman asked, affronted. Then her voice grew cunning as she asked, "Looking for a nurse, are you, my fine sir? Why? Is your leg bothering you? How much are you willing to pay to find one?"

William reached into his pockets and slapped a gold coin onto the table. "To help my friend," he said.

It disappeared into the woman's hand almost instantly. She smiled at Kepley. "This way, sir. Come along and I'll find you your nurse."

"Come along," he called to William.

That took her aback. "You want to bring him, too?" she asked. "That will cost you extra, sir."

William didn't hesitate but drew out several gold coins—all of which he slapped onto the table. They disappeared as quickly as the first.

The old woman shrugged. "Just as you choose, sirs. Just as you choose."

She led them through to the back of the inn and up the stairs. Larkin, standing by the doorway, watched them with narrowed, somewhat puzzled eyes. Those nearby were careful to pay no attention to the direction of his gaze and tried, instead, to ease away from him.

Meanwhile, the two men and the woman, paused at the top of the first flight of stairs. "Would you be wanting a young nurse, sir, or an older one?" she asked.

"You, madam, we want you," William said.

"Aye, you, ma'am. You remind me of my old nurse," Kepley added, slurring his words as though still drunk.

She started to object, but then apparently thought of the

coins they'd given her, and she shrugged. "It's been a while, sirs, but just as you wish."

They went all the way to the top floor and she unlocked a door at the end of the hall. No one said a word until they were inside and the door safely locked behind them. The old woman lit a lamp and started to turn back to them.

But in less than a moment William had her arms pinned behind her. "Now," he said, "I think you will answer a few questions for us."

"And don't scream or we'll have to knock you on the head," Kepley warned. "My cane makes a handy weapon."

It was an absurd threat, but she didn't think so. She looked frightened, so William pressed their advantage. "Where are the two ladies you had abducted today?" he demanded.

The woman, who had begun to curse loudly and fluently, now went very still. "How much are you willing to pay to get them back?" she asked.

"What hurt are you willing to risk if you don't tell us?" Kepley countered.

"Hurt me and you'll never see them again. My partner will throttle 'em and drop 'em in the river, quick as a wink," she spat back.

Rivendale let her go and pushed her into the only chair in the room. The two men gathered around her.

"We'll offer you a deal," William said. "You take us to the ladies and we won't hurt you. Refuse and, well, you'll discover how desperate a man can be."

She cursed them some more. And tried to negotiate. But in the end she agreed to lead them to where the two ladies were to be found.

"You'll have to persuade me partner too," she warned.

"We shall," William said grimly.

She grumbled, but led them down the stairs and out the back way. Only Larkin noticed and followed, and they did not notice him. They went through some darkened alleyways that twisted and turned and finally stopped outside a large, dark building. A man was waiting there, and he clearly recognized their guide. He had been lounging against the wall and straightened at the sight of the two men with the woman.

"Here now, what are they doing here?" he demanded of her, with some alarm in his voice.

"They'll pay us well for them ladies we *found* today," she told him, emphasizing the word "found."

The man was not a fool. "Oh, aye, found," the man agreed. "Didn't know what to do wif 'em, we didn't."

"Of course not," a voice behind them agreed sardonically.

William and Kepley turned to see Sir Robert and the Runner standing there. "His informant told us to look here," Stamford said wryly, with a nod toward the Runner.

"'Ere now! Don't be thinking to escape! Open the door, and be quick about it," the Runner said curtly to the man and woman who started to edge away toward the corner of the building.

With a muttered curse, the man did so, and then indicated the others should precede him. "Oh, no," William said to the man and the woman. "We're not pigeons for the plucking. The two of you go first."

Grumbling, the woman took a lantern off the shelf and lit it. William took another and lit that one, determined that she should not have the only light in the place. Behind them, still unnoticed, Larkin watched and nodded to himself, then slipped away. He knew Granny and the doctor very well, he did. They could handle three toffs and a Runner with no problem. Bottom of the river they'd be, and in quick order. And if not, well, he didn't want to be hanging about to be noticed.

Inside, Granny and the doctor led Stamford, Kepley, Rivendale, and the Runner down a flight of stairs and into a room—an empty room.

The moment that fact registered on William, he turned on the pair. "Where are they?" he demanded. "What sort of sham are you pulling here?"

"None!" the woman protested.

"They was here the last time we looked," the man added, spreading his hands. "And there's been someone guarding this door the whole time."

Stamford offered more money, and the Runner spoke a number of threats, but they couldn't budge the two. Finally it became clear the pair were baffled.

"Was there any other way out?" William demanded.

"Only into the river," the old woman said.

"A trapdoor. And like she said, it only goes down to the river," the man added reluctantly. "But they couldn't have gone that way. Not unless you think they thought they could swim to shore in them heavy skirts of theirs."

"Show me," William persisted.

The man lifted the trapdoor. The inky water swirled below. He seemed to be looking for something and couldn't see it.

"I know the river 'ereabouts," the Runner said. "If they went that way, me lord, they'd be swept away by the current. In their skirts they'd not 'ave a chance."

Slowly, William let the trapdoor fall shut again. His face was blank as he stared at the pair.

"Must have been terrible desperate to take that way out," the Runner observed.

"Can we bring charges?" William demanded.

The Runner considered the matter. "P'rhaps," he said. "We did all 'ear them admit to having them ladies 'ere. At the very least, they'll likely spend a night in jail."

"It's the least they deserve," Kepley said, with scarcely suppressed emotion.

The Runner nodded, his own face sober as he turned to the pair. "Come along, now."

They tried to run, but William immediately blocked their

way. He thrust the woman toward Stamford, and then, with the lantern in his left hand, he landed a blow in the man's face with his right. It was enough to cause the fellow to stagger into the Runner's waiting embrace. Together, Stamford and the Runner forced the pair up the stairs, as Rivendale and Kepley held the lanterns to light their way.

Outside, a small crowd had gathered. Some would have objected and tried to stop them, but William pulled a pistol from his pocket. "I've just learned my wife is dead," he said. "The first man who tries to interfere will get shot. I've no reason not to shoot."

They backed away, no one willing to be the one to risk testing William's determination or the wild look in his eyes. So they continued to back away, down the street—Rivendale, Kepley, Stamford, the Runner, and their two prisoners. William kept his pistol at the ready.

With no more than one or two mistaken turns, they reached the point where the carriage should have been waiting. It wasn't. Stamford cursed.

"A right proper end to the evening this is," the Runner said in disgust.

"Hail a hackney," William said tersely. "We'd best not waste time looking for your carriage, not here. Who knows when someone will find their courage and try to rescue this disgraceful pair? I'll not have them get off that way."

It was Kepley who spotted the hackney and flagged it down. They hastily bundled the prisoners inside and then climbed in themselves.

"Straight to Bow Street," the Runner ordered.

Moments later they were on their way.

At Bow Street, the pair was taken away. The Runner, Rivendale, Kepley, and Sir Robert each gave a report to the magistrate, and then they were free to leave.

"What now?" Kepley asked. "Do we go back to the docks to try to find your carriage? And to ask if anyone has seen Miss Winsham or Lady Rivendale?"

"Of course," William said grimly, not waiting for Stamford's reply.

"It's been a long evening," the Runner objected. "And a right busy one! It ain't wise for you to show your faces down there again—leastwise not so soon arter what we just done. If you'll trust me to the task, I'll go and look for your carriage and send it to you. Why don't you gentlemen go home? Likely if there is word about the ladies, I'll hear it better on me own, anyway."

Stamford and Rivendale both hesitated. However sensible the advice, they could not let go of the desire to check for themselves if there was any chance the two women had survived. Apparently the Runner could see it in their faces, for he said, as though suddenly struck by the thought, "P'rhaps yer ladies found the carriage. The coachman would 'ave taken 'em 'ome, wouldn't 'e?"

Stamford and Rivendale looked at each other. "I suppose it's possible," William said slowly.

"We would not lose so very much time by checking," Kepley added.

"Good," the Runner said. "Now go 'ome and let me do me job!"

Reluctantly they agreed. The hackney carriage was still waiting, for Stamford had paid the man generously to do so, with a promise of more to come. They rattled along at a brisk pace through the now almost empty streets.

"Do you think it possible they are safely at home?" William asked.

Stamford sighed. "I cannot think why else my coachman would have deserted his post. And yet, you saw that trapdoor with the river below. How could they have survived a plunge into that water? But we shall see. If they did find my coachman, he will have taken them to my house. We will stop there first."

"And if they are not there?" Kepley asked.

Neither Sir Robert nor Rivendale bothered to answer.

The moment the carriage drew to a halt, both men were out of it and up the steps.

"Wait for us!" Stamford commanded the hackney driver curtly.

Kepley followed more slowly. The front door opened and Stamford's majordomo, Wilkins, hurried down the steps to greet them.

"They're home, sir," he said. "Miss Winsham and Lady Rivendale and a young person. All safe and sound, sir!"

"Thank God for that!" William murmured.

Stamford turned to the hackney driver and tossed him up the promised fare. "You may go," he said. "All is well here, after all."

The man tipped his hand to his hat and drove away, but neither Stamford nor William nor Kepley stayed to see him go. They were already inside the house, tossing aside their hats and gloves, and then hurrying up the stairs to the drawing room where Wilkins said the ladies were drinking tea and eating a tidy, if belated, dinner.

The three men halted in the doorway of the drawing room, startled by the sight that met their eyes. Tessa and Aunt Margaret looked as elegant as if nothing more untoward than a stroll through the park had occurred.

Miss Winsham noticed them first. "Well? Found your way back here, have you? Come in and sit down. I haven't the patience to tell this story more than once."

"You look," Rivendale said carefully, as he came toward them, "quite well. Clearly you are both all right."

"Were we mistaken in thinking you were in danger?" Stamford added, patently bewildered.

"You ought to have seen them when they first arrived," Alex replied, with a stern frown at her husband.

"They were covered with mud!" Lisbeth added eagerly. "And their gowns were torn. And they were famished, positively famished!"

"So I see," William said dryly. "When you are ready, Sir

Robert and Kepley and I should like to hear the entire
story."

"Well, sit down," Miss Winsham said tartly. "This will
take some time. And then the three of you can tell us what
nonsense you have been up to, down by the docks tonight!
What in the world possessed you to go there? Don't you
know how dangerous a place it can be?"

Chapter 22

Down by the river, Larkin pounded a wall with his fist in frustration. Not only had Granny and the doctor failed to take care of the three toffs and the Runner, but that interfering woman and her companion had gotten away as well. Suddenly he lifted his head. He heard the sound of a carriage. A chance for easy pickings, perhaps?

Ah, even better. It was the same carriage as before. And that meant someone would be back, and he'd have his shot at revenge. One thing was certain: someone would pay for tonight's bungling.

That was odd. The carriage came to a halt where it had stood before. But no one got out. Waiting for the men, perhaps? Had they come back again? When? How had he missed it? Or did the coachman not know they were gone?

Well, no matter. He would wait and see what transpired. Larkin leaned back further into the shadows. Whomever the coachman meant to wait for, he would wait for them as well. No one came into his part of town without paying a price.

He hoped it would be them gentlemen what had brought a Runner with them. Granny and the doctor might not have noticed in time, but he had. And he didn't like it, not one bit. No more than he liked that lady coming here to try to take away children.

That was his lay, taking away children. Selling them, too, for a pretty profit elsewhere. Some of them brought a nice

price, they did. And it was precisely the ones who did that
the lady was taking away from here! Tonight she'd taken
one of the street drabs, too. A girl named Mary he could depend upon to tell him what he wanted to know.

She got afraid easily, did Mary. Which made her very
useful to him. And it made it a pleasure for him to deal with
her. But now that lady had taken her away! Well, if Granny
and the doctor had failed to stop her, he would just have to
do it himself. After he took care of the toffs!

A sound distracted him. It seemed to be coming from
around the corner, a direction that would take him out of
sight of the carriage. Larkin hesitated. He really did not
wish to miss his chance at the toffs. On the other hand, this
was his part of town and he liked to keep an eye on things
himself. Especially since it sounded as if money was
changing hands.

Perhaps a moment or two away from the carriage
wouldn't matter. It would take longer than that for the toffs
to cross any of these streets to get to it, even if they was
still hanging about, which they might not be. And if money
was changing hands, Larkin meant to see if he could get
some of it.

So he slipped backward around the corner, careful to
keep his eyes on the carriage in front of him, scanning the
street for signs of the toffs even as he listened to the sounds
behind him. Suddenly he came face-to-face with a Bow
Street Runner—and a pistol pointed straight at him.

"Now what have we here?" the Runner asked softly. "If
it isn't Larkin. Been looking for you, I has. Little matter of
murder, a month or so ago. Gen'lemun what oughtn't t've
been down 'ere but 'e was. And I been thinking. Thinking
maybe t'weren't Granny and the doctor what thought of
taking them ladies. Maybe someone else put the notion in
their 'eads. And who better than you, Larkin? I saw you
when we took 'em away. Powerful interested you was."

Larkin tried to run, but the Runner was quicker. Which

he ought to have been, given that's what he was called, Larkin thought bitterly. Still, he didn't go easily. He landed a nice blow to the Runner's face, and might have gotten away then, but he ran into the street and the coachman moved to block his way. The next thing he knew, Larkin was being shoved into the toff's carriage and taken to Bow Street. Which would have been bad enough even without the Runner gloating, but with it was well nigh intolerable.

"Been waiting to catch you a long time," the Runner gloated. "A long time, indeed. Meself, I'll earn a tidy reward for this, I will."

Larkin cursed the Runner, and that only made the fellow laugh harder. It was a short and yet entirely too long journey, from his point of view. Especially since the end of it was likely to be the hangman's noose. The only thing that brought the least hint of humor to his eyes was wondering what the toffs would think when they found that their carriage had disappeared again.

That was a question the coachman was asking himself up on the box. It was all very well to be ordered by a Runner to drive him and his prisoner to Bow Street. And he didn't think Sir Robert would mind. But now he'd have to go back to that spot and wait all over again. And then, when Sir Robert did finally show, he'd have to explain to him, and to Lord Rivendale and the other gentleman, where he'd been and what had been going on and hope the delay hadn't put any of them in any danger. All of that was going to take time, and he really had hoped to be home and in his bed by now!

Perhaps the Runner understood something of his dilemma after all, for when they reached Bow Street, he paused to speak to the coachman.

"I'll be straight out again to talk with you, so mind you wait! You'll save yerself some trouble and inconvenience if you do," the Runner said.

"Aye, sir. But Sir Robert—"

"Would want you to wait!" the Runner said at once, cutting him off.

The coachman shrugged. Well, if it was going to be a long night, then it was going to be a long night, and there was nothing to be done about the matter.

But the Runner was out sooner than expected. And he had in his hand a letter. "Give it to Sir Robert," he said. "He'll want to know."

"Oh, to be sure. When I finds Sir Robert," the coachman said with heavy irony.

The Runner looked taken aback, then chuckled. "Oh, aye, that's right. You don't know. Nor do I, now that I think upon it, without I ask you about Lady Stamford. Did they by any chance find you down by the river?" he asked.

It was the coachman's turn to be surprised. "Aye, they did," he said slowly. "And I took them home, thinking that would be what Sir Robert would want."

"Absolutely right," the Runner agreed. "And I sent Sir Robert 'ome thinking he'd find his wife there. So that's where I presume you will find 'im. That's why I asked you to wait. Didn't want you to have to go back near the river, and find yourself waiting for someone who wasn't going to come, if it wasn't needful. And I didn't want to have to chase you down again to tell you Sir Robert was safe, which I'd promised him I would do."

"I do appreciate the news, sir!" the coachman said fervently.

"Good, good. Now just deliver that note to Sir Robert and you'll be done for the night," the Runner promised. "Me? I've a prisoner to see to."

And with that he turned and went back inside, not even waiting to see the coachman drive away.

The Runner was not entirely correct, however. When the coachman arrived at Sir Robert's town house, he did indeed discover that Stamford and the other gentlemen had returned there earlier. When he delivered the note, however, he was not dismissed for the night but rather was told to wait to deliver Lord and Lady Rivendale home.

Upstairs, Stamford read the note, then looked up and smiled grimly. "Bow Street tells me they have captured a man wanted for some time for the murder of a gentleman down near the river. It appears he was also interested in us."

"Who?" Kepley asked.

"Larkin."

The name meant nothing, except to Miss Winsham. She drew in her breath with an audible hiss.

"You know of this man?" Sir Robert asked, with some surprise.

She nodded. "I heard him spoken of, more than once, when I was looking for children in need of rescue. I was told he was not a good man to have as an enemy, and that he would take exception to what I was doing. Did he have the woman and man abduct us?"

"Bow Street thinks so, but they doubt that can ever be proved. Still, they would like you to come and see the fellow tomorrow, and tell them if he is someone you recognize."

"I shall be happy to do so," Miss Winsham said, her voice as grim as Stamford's. "From what I heard, he also was looking for children, but for purposes far different than my own. He sold them to the highest bidder and often took orders for specific types of children. I hope he may hang."

"Yes, well, we all do," Lord Rivendale said, rising to his feet and drawing Tessa with him. "But Sir Robert's carriage is waiting to take us home, so we shall bid you good night, Lady Rivendale and I."

He paused and looked at both Kepley and Stamford. His voice was thick with emotion as he said, "Thank you. For all your help tonight, thank you."

Lord Kepley and Sir Robert nodded. There was no need to say a word, for all three men knew too well what had been at stake tonight. Stamford escorted William and Tessa downstairs and saw them seated in his carriage, while Kepley set off on foot, refusing the offer of a ride.

Sir Robert went back upstairs to Alex. Tonight he was going to hold her very close, he vowed, and tell her, no, he would show his wife, just how dear she was to him, just how deeply he loved her.

In the carriage, Tessa and William looked at one another. Tessa held her breath, hoping he would reach out to her. Instead, he seemed to draw away into the farthest corner of the carriage.

His voice was cold as he said, "You were remarkably foolish today."

"I did what I thought I must," she countered.

"I thought I had lost you," he said, trying hard to keep his voice even.

"I thought myself lost more than once today," Tessa replied. "But I could not abandon Aunt Margaret when I saw her in trouble."

William looked away. "I should dislike to criticize someone so dear to you," he said. "And I must concede that I think Miss Winsham's desire to help unfortunate children to be an admirable one."

"But?" Tessa prompted him.

He looked back at her, and this time he did not try to hide the exasperation in his voice. "But I greatly dislike the notion of the danger in which she places herself!" he said. "And I dislike even more the danger into which she drew you today. I wish Miss Winsham would leave such work to others better suited to it."

"Who?" Tessa asked softly. "Who else would care so deeply? Who else has ever done so?"

And for that he had no answer.

Tessa went on. "I do not like the notion of my Aunt Margaret placing herself in danger. I do not like knowing she may be hurt. But I cannot fault her for doing what matters most to her."

They glared at one another, neither giving way. The ride was a short one, and they did not speak another word until the carriage stopped.

The town house was still ablaze with candles, and Giles was on watch for them, for he opened the door even before they reached the top step. In the drawing room they found Nanny and Anna waiting for them.

"I'm sorry, sir, I could not get Anna to go to sleep," the woman said. "She insisted upon coming down here to wait. I presume she was worried about the both of you."

Anna hugged her father's legs and then turned to hug Tessa. There were tears in the little girl's eyes, and she clung to Tessa as though she would never let her go. Tessa took the child's hand and drew her over to the sofa. There she lifted her onto her lap, and Anna rested her head against Tessa's breast.

William stood looking at them. In spite of his anger about what had happened today, he could not help but be pleased by the change in his daughter's attitude. He thrust his hands into his pocket and, a moment later, exclaimed in surprise, "What the devil?"

"What is it?" Tessa asked.

"This," he said, drawing her locket out of his pocket. "You remember I told you that it was what made us certain you had been abducted? That I found it in the alleyway off the street of dry goods shops?"

"Yes, of course. But I thought you couldn't find it. At Sir Robert's house you said you must have lost it again."

"I thought I had," William said slowly. "Apparently I was mistaken, because here it is."

He held the locket out to Tessa, but Anna reached out for it as well. Tessa let her hold it. But she was not in the least prepared for what happened next.

"Pretty," Anna said softly.

Tessa and William looked at each other in disbelief. Nanny, standing nearby, gave a tiny cry, but she did not move. It was as if she, like the others, was afraid to discover they were mistaken, afraid to alter the miracle that seemed to be occurring.

Slowly Tessa took back the locket and opened it. Then, as she held Anna on her lap, she let the child see how it worked. But Anna wanted the locket to stay open, and for a very long moment, she kept looking back and forth between the locket and Tessa's face and her father.

Finally Anna touched the locket. First she touched one side and said, "Mama." Then she touched the other side and said, "Papa."

The locket seemed to grow warm in her hands, and as Tessa stared at it, over the top of Anna's head, she could have sworn she saw William's face on one side and her own sharing space with a dark-haired beauty on the other.

"Mama," Anna repeated, touching Tessa's hand now. Then she scooted off Tessa's lap and went over to William. "Papa," she said, touching his hand as well.

He knelt down to look her straight in the eye. In a voice that was grave and filled with suppressed emotion he said, "Yes, I am your papa, and Theresa is your new mama."

Anna stared at him. Tessa came over and knelt beside the child too. "I know you loved your mama," she said. "You will always love her. But I hope you may have a place in your heart for me as well. Just a little place?"

Anna began to nod her head. She threw herself first into Tessa's arms and then hugged her father.

Over the child's head, William said to Nanny, "Perhaps she ought to go to bed now. She has had a long and worrisome, exhausting day."

Nanny nodded. "And by the looks of things, so have the pair of you. Come, sweetling," she told Anna. "It's time to put you to bed."

When Anna would have clung to Tessa, she looked the

child straight in the eye and said, "It's all right, Anna. You will see me, and your father, in the morning. For now it is time to sleep."

With obvious reluctance, Anna allowed Nanny to take her hand and lead her toward the stairs up to the nursery. William and Tessa watched them go.

"I thought I would never hear her speak," he said, constraint evident in his voice.

"Nor did I," Tessa admitted, her own voice markedly unsteady. She took a breath and went on, "Today made me realize how precious time is. And the people we care about. It made me realize how grateful I am that I have you and Anna."

But he did not react as she hoped. Instead, he moved several steps away. Over his shoulder he said to her, "Did it? It made me realize the folly of forgetting how little I could bear losing another wife. How little my daughter could cope if anything happened to you. That is why, Theresa, I must forbid you from ever doing anything so foolish as you did today."

"You called me Tessa last night, William," she reminded him softly.

From the way what little she could see of his face turned red, he remembered, but it persuaded him of nothing. "A mistake!" William snapped at her. "It would be better if we returned to the formality of Theresa and Rivendale."

"Better for whom?" Tessa asked softly.

He turned then and looked at her. He could not hide the pain in his eyes as he said, "For both of us!"

Tessa understood his fear. She knew that had their positions been reversed she might have felt the same. But she didn't, and she was determined not to lose him again. She took several steps toward him, even as he backed away. But there was only so far he could go before he stood against the wall and could retreat no further.

"Today," she said, "made me realize how much a part of my heart you are, as well as of my life."

And then, before he could speak or withdraw from her, Tessa stood on tiptoe and cupped his face in her hands as she kissed him. It was a gentle kiss, both a plea and a promise of days and nights of love to come. And he could not help but respond.

When William lifted his head and looked down at Tessa, searching her face for what she might be feeling, she stroked the side of his face and smiled. And this time when she drew his head down for another kiss, it was not a gentle one. It was hungry and urgent and demanding.

"Come upstairs with me," she whispered.

He wanted to refuse, Tessa could see it in his eyes. But he could not. And in the end, with a groan and a muttered curse, William lifted her off her feet and carried her up the flight of stairs. This time he did not stop at her bedchamber. Instead he carried her all the way down the hallway to his.

And when he opened the door to his bedchamber and saw his valet waiting inside, William told the startled fellow, "I shan't be needing you tonight."

"No, sir!" Then the man recovered himself, and he gave Rivendale an impertinent grin as he added, "It's about time you didn't, sir!"

William would have growled something at him, but Tessa stopped him. When the door closed behind the valet and they were alone, she smiled and said, "He is happy for you. Your staff is devoted to you, you know."

"I don't," he answered, biting off each word as he set her down and began to shrug out of his jacket, "wish to speak about the servants. I have other things in mind."

"Oh? What sort of things?" she asked, pretending to an innocence she did not feel.

In answer, William turned her around and began to undo the back of her dress. She shivered as his fingertips traced a trail from her neck all the way down her back. And when he eased the dress off her shoulders, she shivered again.

"Turnabout is only fair," she said, whirling to face him and beginning to undo his shirt.

If Tessa hoped to disconcert him, she was mistaken. He grinned his approval and stood still to let her do as she wished. Her dress slipped lower and he traced the now shockingly low neckline with his fingertips again. He grinned each time she shivered, but there were moments when he shivered too.

Chapter 23

When Tessa went to the nursery early the next morning, she found Anna waiting for her. The moment Tessa stepped into the room, the child came running toward her and reached up to be hugged.

"Good morning," Tessa said, swinging Anna up into the air. "Did you sleep well?"

Anna nodded. She reached out and touched the new chain Tessa's locket was on. "Pretty," she said, echoing her word from the night before. Then, her voice sad, she added, "Mama died. Horses. Carriage. Tree."

Tessa felt her voice catch in her throat. "I know," she said softly. "I'm sorry."

"Go back there?" Anna asked, leaning back so she could see Tessa's face.

"Do you mean that you want to go back there?" asked Tessa cautiously. "Or are you asking me if you must go back there? Because you don't have to, you know."

Anna buried her face against Tessa's neck. "Want to go back," she whispered.

Tessa hugged Anna, then set her back on her feet and crouched down so that she was eye to eye with the child. "I'll talk with your papa, all right?"

Anna nodded, and a very thoughtful Tessa made her way down to the breakfast room, where she found William.

"Good morning, Theresa," he said formally.

She looked at him sadly. "Last night there were moments

when you called me Tessa. Can you not do so this morning as well?"

He flushed but did not answer, clearly very aware of the interested servants. Tessa sighed, but she did not argue. She understood only too well his fear of letting her into his heart. Most of her life she had felt the same. Let him think he could protect himself; she knew better. For now, she had something more important to speak to him about. But she took her time. She filled a plate, settled in the chair opposite his, and began to eat.

"Well?" he said at last. "I cannot believe that you have nothing to say, this morning of all mornings."

Tessa would have smiled, if the matter had not been so grave. "Actually, I do," she admitted. "I saw Anna before I came down to breakfast. She asked to go back to the place where her mama died."

"No!" Rivendale's answer was instinctive, and he was on his feet in seconds. "I will not take her back there! Good God, are you insane? Think of the damage it could do her! Anna has just spoken her first words and you think to take her back to the place where she lost her voice?"

"It is what she wishes, what *she* asked for," Tessa replied, careful to keep her voice soft and calm and even. "I truly think it would help Anna, or I would not ask. I believe it is something she needs to do."

Still he stood staring at her. She could see from his face that he wanted to refuse. But he didn't. At least not outright. Instead he asked, his voice full of pain, "And what if it makes matters worse?"

"What if it helps? What if it finally sets Anna free from whatever demons have been haunting her this past year?" Tessa countered.

Slowly Rivendale sat down. His face was set in grim lines, and he was silent for a very long time, but in the end, reluctantly, he said, "I still think you are mad, but I cannot ignore the chance that you might be right. When did you mean for us to go?"

"If she still wishes to do so, then tomorrow morning," Tessa replied, careful not to let any hint of triumph escape into her voice or her expression. "That will give us time to pack whatever we need to take with us. And time for Anna to change her mind."

William nodded. "Very well," he said. "We leave tomorrow morning. And I pray to God you are not mistaken in what you believe we ought to do!"

Since that was a hope Tessa devoutly shared, she did not even try to answer. Nor did she try to stop him when he left the breakfast room. To go back to his estate would be difficult not only for Anna but for William as well. He would once again have to visit the spot where he had lost his beloved wife. That would not, could not, be easy for anyone.

Lord Rivendale's estate was several hours away from London. They arrived late the next afternoon, much to the surprise of William's mother and uncle.

"I am delighted to see you, of course," Lady Rivendale said, greeting her son with an affectionate hug. "But why did you not let us know you were coming, so that we could prepare rooms for all of you?"

As William's mother enfolded her in a tight embrace as well, Tessa tried to explain. "We did not know ourselves, for certain, until this morning. It was Anna. She wanted to come."

At that, Lady Rivendale blinked in surprise and reached down to lift up her granddaughter. Anna clung tightly, then pushed away.

"Mama," Anna said, her voice still scratchy from disuse. "Want to see where Mama died."

"Good Lord! Did that child just speak?" Cecil Rivendale could not help but exclaim.

Tessa turned to him. In as matter-of-fact a voice as she could manage she said, "Yes, Anna spoke her first words a couple of days ago. We are delighted to discover what a lovely voice she has."

"You have worked miracles!" Lady Rivendale said to Tessa.

"And how do you know that I did not work the miracle?" William demanded, pretending outraged pride.

His mother looked at him thoughtfully. "Perhaps," she conceded. "But since you did not succeed in an entire year, and Anna has spoken such a short time after your marriage, I cannot help but presume that it is Theresa who has made such a difference to my granddaughter."

But Anna had had enough of such talk. She tugged at the shoulder of Lady Rivendale's elegant gown. When she had her grandmother's attention, she said, "Cake?"

Lady Rivendale laughed. "Absolutely right!" she said. "That's what's important—cake! Come, we shall send to the kitchen for tea and cake at once. It is not every day, after all, that I get to entertain my grandchild. You must come and tell me all about London and what you have been doing since I left."

Tessa and William drew closer together, words unable to express what they felt, the joy in seeing Anna begin to answer her grandmother. Nearby, even Cecil seemed overcome with unaccustomed emotion.

He cleared his throat and said gruffly, "Never thought to see the day. Your mother, m'boy, thought we never would. Said we ought to resign ourselves. Glad she was wrong. Glad to see you here, too. Thought it a mistake for you to stay away so long."

Then, before either Tessa or William could ask Cecil Rivendale what he meant, the older man turned and disappeared back into the library. He shut the door with a distinct thump that signaled his wish to be left alone.

"Come, Theresa. We had best see what my daughter is

telling my mother," William said, clearing his own throat first. "I do not wish Anna to plague her."

"In a moment," Tessa countered. She hesitated, then decided to press on. "I know it must be difficult for you to be here. If you wish, I could go with Anna to the spot where your wife died. You need not come unless you wish."

He shook his head. "I have come this far, I will come the rest of the way as well." Then, determined to change the mood, he said lightly, "Come, or my daughter will have eaten all the cake, and that, I promise you, is not something I can contemplate with equanimity!"

Tessa laughed, as he meant her to, and went with him to the drawing room. It would have been too much to say that Anna was speaking with any degree of animation. The words came out in fits and starts, haltingly much of the time. But she spoke. She told Lady Rivendale about London and her favorite toys. She even spoke of Tessa's disappearance two days earlier. That caused Lady Rivendale to turn to her son and his wife with a distinct question upon her face.

Tessa answered hastily, trying to keep her voice light as she said, "Yes, er, there was a misunderstanding. Someone wished to kidnap my aunt, Miss Winsham, and I, er, got caught up with her by mistake. But we managed to escape, and William and his friends managed to capture the villains, so everything is fine now."

"Indeed," Lady Rivendale said in a dry voice that left neither her son nor Tessa in any doubt that the conversation would be continued later, when Anna was not present. She turned back to her granddaughter. "I have been thinking, Anna, that perhaps while you are here you would like to see your other grandparents."

William started, but he could not object. Indeed, he had the grace to say, "Yes, no doubt they would also be happy to hear her speak again."

Lady Rivendale nodded. "I shall send around a note

inviting them to call on us tomorrow. Perhaps you would like to take it over, William?"

"No, no," he said hastily, actually backing away from his mother and toward the door as he answered. "I, er, Theresa and I are tired. I think we shall retire to our rooms. We shall see you at dinner, Mama."

He tugged at Tessa's hand, but she paused to speak to Anna first. "Do you mind if we leave you with your grandmother and go and rest?" she asked.

Anna shook her head. Tessa gave her a hug, then allowed William to lead her out of the room. Indeed, she could not say she was sorry to have the chance to look around. It was evident from the way he pointed out some of the features of the house, as they went upstairs, that William was proud of his home estate. That made it all the sadder that he had exiled himself for this whole past year.

She did not press him to talk about anything and, perversely, that made William more loquacious than he might otherwise have been. "These are the portraits of my ancestors," he said when they reached the upstairs gallery. "We Rivendales have been in this house for hundreds of years. The wood-paneled foyer was the center hall when this manor house was first built. Since then it has been a tradition that each new Lord Rivendale adds something significant to the house."

"What have you added?" Tessa asked quietly.

"Nothing."

The word was curt, meant to cut off all discussion. But it didn't work that way. Tessa waited several moments, then said, in a calm and even conversational voice, "Well, what would you like to add?"

"I don't know."

There was a sense of despair in the voice, and it made Tessa's own heart ache. She hoped that tomorrow's expedition to see the site of his first wife's death might bring him some peace, just as she hoped it would do the same for

Anna. But until then she could think of nothing to do that might help, except to love him. And once they reached the bedroom assigned to them, she did just that.

They were a trifle late to dinner, but neither Cecil Rivendale nor William's mother seemed to mind. Indeed, had she not known better, Tessa would have said that Lady Rivendale winked at her before she led them all in to the table.

Chapter 24

It was a bright, sunny day, at odds with the mood of the party that set out for the isolated spot on Rivendale's estate where a carriage crash had changed everyone's lives a little over one year earlier.

It was a surprisingly large party that went there. Tessa and William and Anna rode in a closed carriage. Lady Rivendale and Cecil Rivendale rode in a curricle. Even the late Lady Rivendale's parents, Lord and Lady Lofton, met them at the ill-fated spot.

"For we've as much curiosity as anyone as to what Anna will say or do," they explained.

Only Anna seemed unaware of the atmosphere among the group. Tessa held William's hand tightly as the child let go of theirs and walked forward. It was still possible to see the gash in the tree trunk where Juliet's curricle had collided with it, smashing into pieces, killing Juliet, and throwing Anna some distance away.

"What a damnable shame," Cecil said, his eyes suspiciously bright.

"I ought never to have bought that curricle and those horses for Juliet," William said grimly. "But I had no notion they were so high-strung, or that they would run away with her! They were always so docile before."

Anna must have heard her father, for she turned and said, her eyes and expression grave, her voice scarcely a whisper, "Mama told me not to tell. Mama made them go fast. Every time. Mama wanted to crash the carriage."

For a long moment there was silence. Then Lady Rivendale went over to the child. "You must be mistaken," she said. "Your mother would not have wanted such an accident to occur. She would have known the danger to both of you."

"She said we would be with the angels. But she said not to tell. She said everyone would know when it was done. But you didn't know. You cried and cried, but Mama wanted this," Anna said earnestly.

"It is not possible," William said angrily. "Why would she have done such a thing?"

It was Juliet's parents who had the answer. Their faces were bleak as they came forward to stand beside Rivendale. "She wasn't the first," Juliet's mother said softly. "There have been too many Loftons who fell prey to melancholy and made such a choice. I knew she was unhappy, but I had no notion it was this bad."

"Why didn't you tell us?" Lady Rivendale demanded.

Lord Lofton looked at her, his eyes as bleak as Anna's had ever been. "Would you have talked about such a thing? To be sure, Juliet was sad sometimes as a girl. But she seemed so happy when your son asked to marry her. We really thought it would be all right."

"Was it . . . was it something I did? Or failed to do?" William asked, his voice full of constraint.

Lady Lofton turned to him. "Oh, no! No, William!" She paused, and her own voice was constrained as she made herself go on. "Juliet was such a foolish young woman. I am her mother, but I cannot forgive her for what she did to you. I do not know why she could not find contentment with you, Rivendale, but it was her own choices that drove her to desperation. She once said that had she been capable of loving any man, that man would have been you. But she could not. And that was her greatest tragedy."

William could not answer. Instead, he moved a little

apart. Tessa went to put a hand on his shoulder. He turned to her and went into the arms she held open to him. Behind them, they could hear voices, as the others discussed what had happened, but Tessa and William clung to one another in silence. There were no words for what he felt, nor any for her to comfort him. Not yet. That might come later. For now, there was simply an overwhelming grief.

As if they understood, the others began to move away. Lady Rivendale came over long enough to say, "We shall leave our curricle for you. The rest of us are returning to the house. We shall see you there, when you are ready."

When they were alone, William let go of Tessa and walked over to touch the gash in the tree. She stood where she was, just watching. This was a journey he had to make himself. When he was ready, he would come back to her. And she would be waiting.

"I should have known something was wrong," he said, his voice coming as if from a distance.

"How?"

"I thought it was just me. That Juliet was disenchanted just with me. I had no notion it was more than that. She always seemed so gay! There was never an invitation she could refuse. Never a dance not to be danced. Except when she would fight with me and then shut herself up in her room. I thought her unhappiness then was my fault."

"And that is why you fear to let me into your heart," Tessa said quietly. "Because you are afraid you will lose me as well. But you lose me every day if you don't."

He looked at her then, and the anguish in his eyes was almost more than she could bear. Still, she willed herself to stand where she was, to let him come to her.

"How?" he asked. "How am I supposed to let you into my heart, when I could lose you as well?"

"I am not Juliet," Tessa countered, her voice firm and clear, betraying none of the emotions she felt. "How do you let me in? With a leap of faith. You simply do. And in time the fear diminishes. In time you begin to believe the truth—that we can be happy together. That it is safe to love."

"But what if I cannot be the man you want?"

"What if you are?" Tessa leaned back against the tree behind her, to keep herself from going to him. "I do not ask perfection, no nor need it either. I am not Juliet. I will not seek faster horses or other men or an accident to still an inner pain."

Now he came toward her, and still Tessa waited for him. He stopped a few feet away. "So you think I could be the man you want?" he asked with his head tilted to one side.

"I know that you are."

"How?"

Tessa searched for the words that would persuade him. At last she said, "You found me. When Aunt Margaret and I were kidnapped, you found us. And when you most wanted to keep me out of your heart, you couldn't do so. You fought to find a way to help Anna speak. What more could I want of the man I love? What more could I ask him to do?"

He seemed stunned. He took another step forward and reached out his hand toward her. "You . . . love me?" he asked, the uncertainty evident in his voice.

Tessa put her hand in his. It trembled, but she didn't care. This was her life, her love she was fighting for. "Yes," she said softly, a wry smile on her face, "I love you. I can't tell you precisely why or when it happened, but it did. Even though I knew you didn't want me to. Even though I knew you might not be able to love me back."

His hand gripped hers tightly now. He pulled her toward him and she came without protest. This was what she wanted, too. And when her body was touching his, Tessa pulled her hand free and wound both her arms around his neck.

"I will always love you," she said. "Forever and ever. Because to stop loving you would be to stop breathing, to stop living."

And then Tessa kissed him. Kissed him with all the passion he had taught her to feel. Until William wrapped his arms around her and pulled her tight in a fierce hug, as though he never meant to let her go.

"I love you," he whispered into her hair. "God help me, I never meant to love you, but I do."

Tessa pulled back and looked at him with mock severity. "Then why," she asked in mock exasperation, as she pretended to scold him, "are we arguing?"

He grinned unrepentantly at her and kissed the tip of her nose. "Because we are both stubborn people and cannot help ourselves?" He paused and looked around, as though suddenly realizing how much time had passed. "I think, Tessa," he said, "that we had better go back to the house before my mother decides to send out a search party for us!"

She stared at him. "You called me Tessa."

"Did I?" he countered lightly, drawing her toward the curricle where the horses stood waiting patiently.

She nodded.

"Do you object?" he asked, as he handed her up into the curricle and then gathered up the reins.

Tessa shook her head. "Does that mean I can finally call you William, without you stopping me every other time to complain?" she teased, as he set the horses going.

"Would it matter if I did?"

"No."

He was silent a moment. Then he asked quietly, "Tell me your greatest fear. I would like to help ease yours, as you have just eased mine."

"You know what it is."

"To go out and about in public?"

"Yes."

"But are you truly so afraid of that?" William asked with a frown. "I had thought that perhaps you were becoming accustomed to doing so, even, perhaps, beginning to enjoy it."

Tessa started to disagree, but didn't. It had been a long time, she realized, since she had stopped to consider the matter, or whether her sentiments had undergone a change. And now she realized that they had.

"My father," she said slowly, "always used to tell me that I was a foolish girl. That I embarrassed him simply by my presence in a room with his friends. I used to cry myself to sleep over those unkind words."

"Did it never occur to you," William asked, "that perhaps your father was trying to protect you?"

"Protect me? How? With cruelty?"

"With giving you reason to avoid his friends," he answered gently. "Recollect that your father's friends were not the kindest of men, no, nor all gentlemen either. He may have feared how they were beginning to look at you, and wanted to make certain you avoided them."

Tessa was silent for a very long moment. At last she said, "I had not considered such a thing. I only thought him both cruel and truthful. Do you really think he might have meant to protect me?"

William gave an exasperated snort of disgust. "Trust me, Tessa, when I tell you that no one—no one—could possibly find your company embarrassing! Your father must have been trying to protect you. Either that or he was an utter fool and ought to have been trying to protect you. Either way, you need not regard what he said as anything other than nonsense!"

Tessa leaned her head against William's shoulder, unaccountably reassured by what he had said. "I think you may be right," she said. "And if you are not, I never wish to discover the truth. Papa ought to have valued me, whether he did so or not!"

"Oh, good," William said with mock satisfaction. "Now I can ask you to start hosting large dinner parties for me— just as I always wanted. No more than fifty people or so at a time, of course."

Tessa swatted him on the sleeve at this reminder of her foolishness when he had asked her to marry him. "Not that many people," she said. "But I must confess that the notion of setting covers for ten no longer distresses me. I should like to begin to entertain our friends."

"I should like that as well," he said, his voice sober and honest now.

"Perhaps we could stay long enough to host some of your neighbors here?" Tessa suggested. She saw his instinctive gesture of refusal and went on quickly, before he could voice those objections aloud. "I make no doubt they wanted to and tried to offer you their condolences when Juliet died. But I doubt you could hear it then. Give them the chance to tell you again, now."

He wanted to refuse, she could see it in the way he held himself so rigid, in the way he looked straight ahead, and in the way the muscles quivered about his mouth. Even the horses seemed restless under his touch, and Tessa was grateful they were almost at the house.

But she was mistaken. He had more resolution than she expected, and in the end he sighed and said, "Whatever you think best. If we are ever to come back here again, we will need to be on speaking terms with our neighbors. And when Anna is older it will matter even more. Very well. Arrange it with my mother. Between the two of you, I've no doubt you will manage wondrously well."

Tessa was shrewd enough not to say another word. She simply let William hand her down from the curricle as a groom ran forward to take the reins from him. She didn't even notice that her locket was once again gone. If she had, she would have remembered that Alex had also lost it for good, once she no longer needed it. She would have understood that soon it would be Lisbeth's turn. Whatever Aunt Margaret might say, Tessa knew that it really was magical. As magical as anything she might dream up for any one of her stories.

Epilogue

Anna peered at her new baby brother. "He looks very wrinkled," she said, wrinkling up her own nose.

Tessa laughed. "So did you, no doubt, when you were born."

"Oh, no, I never looked like that, I am certain I didn't! I have always been pretty, haven't I, Papa?" Anna appealed to her father.

It was William's turn to laugh. He lifted her up and pretended to study her. "I think you may have looked like that once. But it passed so quickly that I have forgotten."

"Can I hold him?" Anna begged.

"Perhaps later," an older woman said from behind Anna. "For now it is time to go back to your lessons. You promised that you would do so, without argument, if I let you come and see the baby."

"I don't like having a governess," Anna protested to her parents.

They merely regarded her with a steady gaze, and she reluctantly turned to go. "Very well." Then, with a haughty air, she said to the governess, "You are quite right. A promise is a promise."

Indeed, despite her stated objection to the notion of a governess, Anna took the woman's hand willingly. And went with her back upstairs.

When they were gone, William sat on the bed beside his

wife. The baby she was holding began to cry and Tessa
eased open her robe to feed him.

"Some would say you ought not to do that," William
teased her. "They would say I ought to hire a wet nurse to
do it for you."

"And do you think so?" Tessa asked. "Not that I should
allow it, you understand, but is that what you would truly
prefer?"

He smiled, at both her and the baby. He even began to
stroke his son's cheek. "No, I should prefer that you do
whatever you wish, whatever you think best."

"That is a very wise answer," she told him tartly.

William pushed the hair back from her forehead. "Of
course it is," he agreed smugly. Then he added, in an
offhanded way, "I have a surprise for you. I wonder if you
are recovered enough to have it?"

"William?"

It was a warning, definitely a warning, and William took
it as such. "I shall be right back," he said and then promptly
disappeared from the room.

Tessa muttered to herself something about foolish men,
but then she became absorbed once again in the joy of having her son at her breast. Indeed, she was so caught up in
the sight of the baby and the feel of him that she did not notice at first when William returned.

He stood in the doorway watching for a long moment,
and straightened up to come forward only when she looked
up and realized he was there. He looked oddly awkward.
Whatever he had for Tessa, he held it behind his back.

"I wanted to replace your locket," William told her, "but
Miss Winsham said it could not be done. She said that it
was Lisbeth's turn to have it anyway."

"Never mind," Tessa told her bewildered husband with a
smile, as she remembered how the locket had come to her
after Alex's turn and knowing that Aunt Margaret was right.

"It doesn't matter anymore. Come and tell me, instead, the surprise you do have for me."

William colored up and seemed to shift awkwardly from one foot to another. "It isn't something I can tell, precisely. That is, I, er, I *hope* you will be pleased. It seemed the best thing I could do for you."

"Will you," Tessa said from between clenched teeth, "just be done with it and show me the surprise?"

Rivendale came forward and sat on the bed, careful to set the surprise down behind him, out of her sight. "Let me take the baby first. Then I will give you your surprise, and you won't need to worry that he will do damage to it."

"Wise precaution," Tessa agreed, handing over the now very sleepy baby.

William took the child and cradled him against his chest. With his free hand, he reached behind and brought around two volumes, which he handed to Tessa. "I think you will like these," he said in a careless voice.

Puzzled, Tessa took the books. She opened the first one and gasped at the sight that met her eyes. She looked up at William. Her voice shook as she said, "This looks like one of my stories. But how did this publisher get hold of my manuscript? And did he alter it?"

This last was said suspiciously. Tessa began to turn the pages quickly, wanting to know. William put a hand on the open book to stop her.

"I gave the publisher your manuscripts. And made certain that he understood the consequences should he dare try to alter a word you wrote without your permission. These volumes are the results."

"But Mr. Plimpton—"

"Mr. Plimpton," William said, with no little satisfaction, "has been persuaded to drop all claims to any of your work, now and in the future. He also has been made to understand that if he attempts in any way to interfere with this publisher, or the public's acceptance of your books, then he will regret it. He was most cooperative when I last spoke with him."

"I think," Tessa said, beginning to smile, "that it might be just as well if I didn't ask how you accomplished such a miracle."

"I think you are right," William said gravely, though there was a distinct twinkle in his eyes.

For a long moment they stared at one another.

"The baby's cradle is right by the bed," Tessa whispered.

"Oh? So it is. Perhaps I should put it in the other room so our son can nap undisturbed?"

"Perhaps," she agreed.

William did so and then came back to sit on the bed beside her again. He leaned forward and kissed Tessa.

"How soon?" he asked delicately.

"Three months." She could not hide her crestfallen air.

William laughed softly. Tessa looked at him, taken aback by his patent amusement. "You are happy about that?" she asked.

He only smiled and drew his face close to hers again. "No," he said gently. "I laughed because there are any number of things we can do from now until when we can do that."

Tessa blinked at him. "There are?" she asked, beginning to catch his mood.

"Oh, yes," he assured her.

"Perhaps you should show me what you mean?" she said.

"I think that would be an excellent notion."

And so it was a very scandalized nurse who opened the door sometime later, meaning to check on the baby.

"He's in the other room!" William growled from beneath the hastily grabbed covers.

Her answer was to turn bright red, slam the bedroom door behind her, and hurry down the hallway to the door that led into William's dressing room and the sleeping baby.

Only when she had picked him up and clearly gone down the hallway, so that she was out of hearing, did Tessa and William emerge from under the covers. They looked at one another and began laughing.

"I think," William said, kissing the tip of her nose, "that marrying you was the best thing I have ever done."

"And the best thing I have ever done as well," was Tessa's happy reply.

Author's Note

This is the second in a series of three books about the Barlow sisters. Look for Lisbeth's story next, in *The Soldier's Bride*. What happens when a husband returns almost two years after everyone thought he was dead?

I'd also like to comment about William's first wife. Juliet suffered from what would now be considered manic depression. In the early 19th century, however, such illnesses often went undiagnosed, though people did understand that depression could run in families. But at the time not only was there very little treatment of any kind for mental illness, it often was not recognized as such.

The term manic depression dates from the end of the 19th century and even today it can be a very difficult illness to treat.

Look for news of upcoming books at my Web site: http://www.sff.net/people/april.kihlstrom.

I love hearing from readers. I can be reached by E-mail at april.kihlstrom@sff.net.